Claudia and the Friendship Feud

Other books by
Ann M. Martin

P.S. Longer Letter Later
(written with Paula Danziger)
Leo the Magnificat
Rachel Parker, Kindergarten Show-off
Eleven Kids, One Summer
Ma and Pa Dracula
Yours Turly, Shirley
Ten Kids, No Pets
Slam Book
Just a Summer Romance
Missing Since Monday
With You and Without You
Me and Katie (the Pest)
Stage Fright
Inside Out
Bummer Summer

THE KIDS IN MS. COLMAN'S CLASS series
BABY-SITTERS LITTLE SISTER series
THE BABY-SITTERS CLUB mysteries
THE BABY-SITTERS CLUB series
CALIFORNIA DIARIES series

Friends Forever

Baby-sitters Club

Claudia and the Friendship Feud

Ann M. Martin

AN
APPLE
PAPERBACK

SCHOLASTIC INC.
New York Toronto London Auckland Sydney
Mexico City New Delhi Hong Kong

No part of this publication may be reproduced in whole or in part, or stored in a retrieval system, or transmitted in any form or by any means, electronic, mechanical, photocopying, recording, or otherwise, without written permission of the publisher. For information regarding permission, write to Scholastic Inc., Attention: Permissions Department, 555 Broadway, New York, NY 10012.

ISBN 0-590-52331-7

Copyright © 1999 by Ann M. Martin. All rights reserved. Published by Scholastic Inc. SCHOLASTIC, THE BABY-SITTERS CLUB, APPLE PAPER-BACKS, and associated logos are trademarks and/or registered trademarks of Scholastic Inc.

12 11 10 9 8 7 6 5 4 3 2 1   9/9 0 1 2 3 4/0

Printed in the U.S.A.   40

First Scholastic printing, November 1999

The author gratefully acknowledges
Laura Dower
for her help in
preparing this manuscript.

Claudia and the Friendship Feud

❋ Chapter 1

"Look at *that*!" I gasped, nudging my friend Mary Anne hard with my elbow. She almost dropped her popcorn.

"What?" she whispered back. She was looking at the previews on the movie screen.

"No, Mary Anne. Look at *them*." I pointed to a girl and boy sitting about six rows ahead of us.

Stacey and Jeremy.

Mary Anne leaned closer to me. "Oh, wow. Do you think they know we're here?"

"Who cares?" The last people in the world I wanted to see were Stacey McGill and Jeremy Rudolph. Together.

"Are you okay, Claud?" Mary Anne looked a little worried. "Gosh, I hope Logan isn't here too." She glanced around the theater.

The seven o'clock show of *Lovelocked* was just starting. The movie was supposed to be a tearjerker, a modern-day *Romeo and Juliet*. Kids had been lined up around the block all day to see it.

To be perfectly honest, I wasn't in the mood for a love story, but Mary Anne convinced me to go. She thought a sappy movie would give us the opportunity to have a good cry and not feel too embarrassed about it.

Mary Anne had just broken up with her boyfriend, Logan Bruno, whom she'd been going out with practically forever. Although she knew she'd made the right decision, she was still upset. It was the end of something major.

But believe it or not, my breakup was even more major.

That's because I broke up with Stacey McGill, my best friend.

Well, Stacey *was* my best friend until she stole Jeremy Rudolph away from me.

Jeremy is so cool. He's the new guy in school, tall and kind of shy. He and I hit it off right away. We talked about everything. He told me he liked art, so naturally I thought we would make a cute couple. And Stacey agreed. She even planned our first date.

Boy, did things change fast.

Stacey became a traitor.

That was all I could think of as I crammed a fistful of popcorn into my mouth, my eyes fixed on her and Jeremy. I couldn't hear what they were saying, but I wished that I could.

I remember the exact moment last month when Stacey became my un-best friend.

Poof! She told me Jeremy didn't want to go out with me again. He only wanted to be friends. She was the one he wanted to date.

Poof! I felt my future, the boy of my dreams, vanish as my best friend in the whole wide world *stole* him. And then she said some awful things about me — the kind you just can't take back.

Poof! Good-bye, Jeremy. Good-bye, Stacey.

It still hurt to think about it.

"Try to forget about it," I said to Mary Anne. "I won't let it ruin this movie, and you shouldn't either."

"Actually, maybe we should let Stacey know we're here. It seems rude to just sit here and not say hello."

I grabbed Mary Anne's arm. "What? No way. I can't face her. Not when she's on a *date*. Not with Jeremy."

"Claudia, isn't there some way you guys can

work this out? You and Stacey give each other the silent treatment during BSC meetings, you avoid each other all day at school, and you barely go out because you're afraid you'll run into each other. It's been a month already. A whole month. When are you two going to talk to each other again?"

I rolled my eyes but Mary Anne kept talking.

"You and Stacey are best friends. I don't care what happened. The two of you couldn't possibly have meant all the things you said, could you? You can't let a boy come between you. Isn't this the time of year when we're supposed to be thankful for our friends and family? Aren't we supposed to be celebrating Thanksgiving?"

I sunk back into my seat. Giving thanks was the last thing I felt like doing. As a matter of fact, this was going to be the worst Thanksgiving ever.

I choked down another handful of popcorn and tried to remember exactly what I had said to Stacey during our awful fight. I remembered the words "brainless," "jealous," and "loser," among others.

Mary Anne was right. I knew we hadn't meant to be so cruel. It had just happened.

But now I felt guilty.

If my enemy were Stacey the Traitor, then I was

Claudia the Destroyer. After all, I was the one who'd told Jeremy about Stacey's ex-boyfriend Ethan before she'd had a chance to tell him. That had gotten her into trouble with Jeremy. But it hadn't broken them up. Even *I* didn't have that kind of superpower.

Obviously. Because here they were, cuddling at the movies.

What did Jeremy see in Stacey McGill that I, Claudia Kishi, didn't have?

Maybe Jeremy likes blondes better. Or maybe he wants someone who's good at math.

I watched Jeremy lean into Stacey and whisper into her ear . . . and wondered what he was saying. That could have been *my* ear.

"Earth to Claudia." Mary Anne elbowed me. "The movie's starting. Are you okay? How about some candy?"

She dangled a box of Milk Duds in front of me.

Now, there's a best friend: candy! The only thing I liked better than Milk Duds were chocolate chips, but since they were not available, I happily accepted the chocolate-covered caramels instead.

Junk food *always* helps me feel better.

I opened the box. (Even though my parents don't like me to eat so many sweets, I do. I keep a secret stash of junk food in my bedroom.)

"We'll just pretend they're not here, okay?" Mary Anne said around a mouth full of candy. "We'll just cry into our Milk Duds."

Mary Anne is a good friend. Even with everything that was happening between her and Logan, she still made lots of time for me.

But how could I pretend that Stacey and Jeremy weren't right there in front of me?

Impossible.

Part of me wanted to run as fast as I could until I got home and collapsed onto my bed. Another part of me wanted to keep an eye on Stacey and Jeremy's every move. I wanted to know what made these love-birds tweet. Hey, I didn't like being a spy, but I had no choice.

My genius sister, Janine, would have been proud of me. She always says I can't concentrate or focus on anything. But I was focused today.

After a few minutes, the movie distracted me from Stacey-and-Jeremy watching. But I got confused. I couldn't keep the characters' names or faces straight. And why was this taking place on a desert island? And just what did "lovelocked" mean, anyway?

Thankfully, Mary Anne and her Milk Duds also distracted me. But those feelings of chocolate-and-caramel bliss didn't last long. About ten minutes into the movie, the worst possible thing that could ever happen happened.

I saw Jeremy put his arm around Stacey's shoulders — and squeeze.

I elbowed Mary Anne again, harder than before. This time some of her popcorn fell onto the floor. And a brown clump of Milk Duds flew out of the box.

"What was that?" Mary Anne asked.

"Nothing. Oh, wow. I'm sorry."

I helped her brush off the popcorn kernels that had fallen onto her lap. It was almost impossible to see in the dark.

Uh-oh. I dropped the Milk Duds box and it slid under the seat in front of me. A man in the row behind me tapped me on the shoulder and shushed me. I was mortified. If it hadn't been dark in that theater, Mary Anne would have seen me turn five shades of purple.

"I'm sorry," I whispered to the man.

He grunted back at me, "Kids."

"Just forget about all of it — him included," Mary Anne said, speaking very quietly. "You *are* going to be able to just watch the movie, aren't you?"

Suddenly, I thought of something worse than the man behind us. Stacey and Jeremy.

"Did *they* see us?" I whispered. "Did Stacey and Jeremy turn around when I dropped the box?"

"I don't think anyone heard it . . . except Mr. Friendly behind you."

"Are you positively, absolutely sure they didn't see us?"

"Stop worrying and watch the movie."

But I couldn't. I craned my neck to catch a glimpse of Stacey and Jeremy. Jeremy was whispering in Stacey's ear again, and this time she was laughing. I didn't want to keep looking, but I couldn't help myself. They were being so *obvious*, sitting so close, touching. Didn't they realize that people were watching them?

I closed my eyes. I couldn't look.

I opened my eyes. I wouldn't look.

"*Claudia*," Mary Anne whispered.

I squirmed to get comfortable and tried harder to pay attention. Mary Anne was right. I needed to stop. Now.

The next two hours were the longest of my life.

When *Lovelocked* finally ended, Mary Anne was sobbing. I couldn't figure out if it was because the girl in the movie had lost the guy she loved to some other girl or what.

Maybe Mary Anne was thinking about how much she missed Logan.

While the credits were still rolling, I grabbed her hand and jumped out of the seat. "Let's get out of here," I cried. "I don't want them to see us."

Mary Anne followed me out to the lobby and pulled away. "Claudia, I have to go to the bathroom, okay? Wait for me here. I'll be right out."

As she dashed into the restroom, I ducked behind a pillar.

I couldn't be seen.

There they were.

Stacey and Jeremy.

Jeremy and Stacey.

And they were holding hands. Swinging arms. Laughing.

Stacey looked pretty; I had to admit it. She was wearing this great blue sweater that we'd bought at Bloomingdale's over the summer. And she had arranged painted combs in her hair — ones I had given to her on her last birthday.

I liked her outfit. I would have to remember to tell her that.

If we ever spoke to each other again.

❀ Chapter 2

"Mal says hello." Kristy had just called the Monday meeting of the Baby-sitters Club to order. (The Baby-sitters Club — or BSC — is a business we run. Parents call one number and have four sitters ready to go.)

Kristy was waving a letter in the air. It was from Mallory Pike, former full-time member (and now honorary member) of the club, who was attending boarding school.

"Mal says she's coming back to Stoneybrook for Thanksgiving, but not until Wednesday night," Kristy reported. "And she wants us to know she has a huge crush on some guy in this writing workshop they have with a boys' school."

"Leave it to Mal. A writing workshop crush. That sounds like fun," Mary Anne said.

"I can't wait to see her," I said.

"Yeah — we should all do something together this weekend," Mary Anne suggested. "It would be like old times."

Mary Anne glanced at me and then at Stacey. I could see the wheels turning in her head. She wanted us to stop fighting and start talking again.

Good luck.

Stacey suddenly said, "It would be nice to spend time with Mal and you guys, but I'm sorry . . . I can't."

Mary Anne was disappointed. Kristy nodded. I had nothing to say on this subject.

I knew what was really going on. Stacey had plans, all right. She had plans to blow off Mallory and the rest of the BSC members just to go out with Jeremy again.

"My dad and I are going to be in New York," Stacey started to explain.

"Oh, right. You'll be with your *dad*," I said under my breath. Luckily only Kristy heard me. She shot me a Look.

Okay, I wanted to take back my words as soon as I had said them. But I couldn't help what I felt.

After what had happened at the movies (even though Stacey didn't know I had seen her there), I was mad and sad and jealous all at the same time. Nothing made any sense.

I felt that Stacey had taken Jeremy away from me. And I secretly felt that Jeremy had taken Stacey away from me.

The room was very quiet. Luckily, Kristy broke the ice.

"Sooooo." She clapped her hands as Mary Anne pulled out the BSC notebook. "We should figure out who's going to handle any baby-sitting jobs during Thanksgiving week, right?"

"Sounds good," said Mary Anne. "What's everyone doing for Turkey Day?"

I didn't answer . . . and neither did Stacey.

"Our whole family is going to be together," Kristy said. "Actually, Mom put me on kitchen duty. I'm in charge of the stuffing. I'm actually going to cook."

Mary Anne laughed. "Now, *that's* funny!"

"Not nearly as funny as the fact that my father and Zoey asked if my brothers and I wanted to come out to California for the holidays."

"California?"

"Yes, but now it's too late to make those plans. They asked, like, three days ago. I still think it was cool that they asked, though — I'm sure it was

Zoey's idea. My dad has *never* asked us to spend Thanksgiving with him. Ever. What are *you* going to be doing, Mary Anne?"

"Going to Granny and Pop-Pop's," Mary Anne answered. "Granny's making a huge feast. Maybe that'll get my mind off of Logan."

I glanced at Stacey, who was sitting across the room with her arms crossed. She smiled a half smile, a *fake* smile, at me.

I wanted the meeting to end.

I wished everyone would just get out of my room.

"What about you, Claudia?" Kristy asked.

"What about me?"

Kristy made a funny face at me. "Helloooooo? Anyone home?"

Mary Anne laughed. "For Thanksgiving. What about you, Claudia? Are you going to your aunt's house?"

"N-no," I stammered, "Peaches, Russ, and Lynn are coming to our house . . . with a friend of Peaches' from college."

I wandered into my closet and pulled a box of Oreos from the shelf. My secret stash. "Anyone want a cookie?" I asked, ripping open the package. "Kristy? Mary Anne?"

Since Stacey is diabetic (which means her body has problems with sugar), she couldn't eat these sugary cookies. But I didn't care. I wouldn't offer her a sugar-free snack. Not when she was being so mean.

I stuffed a cookie into my mouth and plopped onto the floor.

Mary Anne and Kristy looked at each other. The only sound was my chewing the Oreo.

Until Stacey spoke.

"What did you say about baby-sitting jobs over the weekend, Kristy? And are we having a Wednesday meeting? Can we talk about that and then go? I have a lot of homework tonight."

Homework? I doubted that. Stacey probably wanted to ditch the meeting so she could meet Jeremy.

The phone rang then.

Kristy grabbed it. "Baby-sitters Club."

Stacey stood up and turned to look out the window. I noticed the photograph in my homemade frame on the wall next to her. The picture had been taken last year. It was of Stacey and me writing sand messages on the beach. Looking happy.

"Hi, Mrs. Pike. How are you?" Kristy chattered into the phone. "Tomorrow? Let me just look at the calendar. I'll call you right back." Kristy turned to the rest of us. "Emergency job at the Pikes' tomorrow afternoon. Mary Anne, who's free to sit?"

Mary Anne checked our club notebook. "Let's see. Claudia is."

I nodded. I wasn't doing anything the next afternoon. My social calendar was not exactly overflowing with events. I looked expectantly at Mary Anne, knowing we'd need a second sitter for the seven Pike kids.

"And you too, Stacey. You're free."

My heart stopped.

Fate was playing a cruel joke. Stacey and me baby-sitting? Together? My stomach was churning.

"But . . ." Stacey and I blurted out at the same time.

". . . I can't." Stacey continued ahead of me. "I have a conflict, Kristy."

"Okay, but I don't think anyone else can do it. Mary Anne has to go to that thing with Sharon tomorrow, and I have to watch David Michael and Emily Michelle. That leaves you and Claudia."

"I'm sorry," Stacey said again. "Please don't be mad."

"I'm not *mad*, Stacey. I understand. But who am I going to get to sit? I'd rather not say no to the

Pikes." Kristy took the pencil from behind her ear.

"Can I do it alone, just this once?" I asked, knowing the answer would be no.

"All of the Pikes? Alone?"

I thought about the triplets and the other four kids and sighed. "I know." If only Mal were coming back a day sooner. Then she could sit with me.

Kristy waved her arm in the air. "I've got it! What about Logan?"

Mary Anne dropped her head into her hands. "Kristy! I can't believe you even said that."

"Oops. Sorry."

Stacey perked up all of a sudden. "Hey, what about Erica Blumberg? She might be free tomorrow."

"Hmm," said Kristy.

Erica and I hang out sometimes at school. She isn't a regular dues-paying member of the BSC, but she might sit for us if we needed extra help. Or when we were desperate — like now.

"You know, that's a good idea, Stacey. She's reliable. Let's give Erica a call." Kristy flipped through the phone book, found the number, and dialed. "Hello, Mrs. Blumberg, is Erica there?" she said into the receiver. After a minute she continued. "Erica? Hi, it's Kristy Thomas. How are you?"

While Kristy explained the situation and made

the baby-sitting arrangements, I watched Stacey and Mary Anne wander over to my bookshelves. They were talking about some English quiz, but I couldn't be bothered listening to them. I'm allergic to tests.

I folded my legs and arms and pondered Stacey's excuses. Was her "conflict" invented? Was she making an excuse so she could see Jeremy without having to admit it to us?

Kristy hung up the phone and gave Mary Anne a high five. "Erica said yes!"

I stuffed another Oreo into my mouth. I knew it was lucky that Erica was free to baby-sit the next day. What a relief.

Across the room, Stacey appeared even more relieved than me.

❀ Chapter 3

On Tuesday morning I almost overslept. It wasn't until I was in homeroom, leaning over to pull out my books, that I noticed I was wearing two different socks. One was bright orange. The other one was brown-striped.

"Very coordinated outfit, Claud," Kristy commented at the lockers after school. "You really know how to make a fashion statement. Your socks match the foliage."

"Ha-ha," I said sarcastically. "Little do you know that I planned it this way. You only wish you were a fashion magnet like me."

Kristy and I always play this game. I'm the artsy, creative one, and Kristy is somewhat more relaxed about her clothes. I like to wear something completely different each day, while Kristy inevitably wears a pair of jeans, sneakers, and a turtleneck.

While we were standing there, Erica Blumberg joined us.

"Cool socks, Claudia," she said. "And in Thanksgiving colors too. I'm impressed."

Kristy snickered and picked up her backpack.

"Have a good time at the Pikes' today," she said. "Sorry to run off, but I have to go pick up David Michael. See you!" She jogged down the stairs.

"So, I've never baby-sat for the Pikes before," Erica confessed. "Are they as much of a nightmare as Mallory always said? What did she call them? Triplet terror?"

"Actually, they're a lot of fun. They're a *lot*, but they're fun. Should we go?"

We grabbed our books and left school, chatting as we walked.

"Where do you live now?" I asked Erica.

"On Elm. Actually, Stacey lives just up the street from my house." Erica paused. "How about you?"

"Bradford Court," I answered. "Close to school. It's an easy walk. Which is good on days like today, since I woke up late."

Erica laughed. "I am Queen of Oversleeping! I don't know why, but it's just impossible for me to get up on time. I'm more of a midday person, I think. I would stay in bed until noon every day if I could."

We walked on, chatting nonstop about which teachers we liked best and which teachers we didn't like at all. Erica told me she couldn't spell to save her life, but she was kind of a math whiz. Just like Stacey.

"I'm not too good at math *or* spelling," I said, a little embarrassed.

"I can help you with homework sometime."

I liked that idea.

"Do you have any brothers or sisters?" I asked her.

"One brother." Erica laughed. "He's trouble."

"I have one sister, Janine, who's in high school . . . and she drives me absolutely crazy. Like, I'm sure we'll have some kind of fight over Thanksgiving. We disagree about almost everything."

"Agree to disagree, that's what my mom always says. Does Janine wear funky Thanksgiving socks too?"

I laughed. "No way. She's too serious for that. She's the brain. I'm the artist."

"I'm jealous. I can't even draw a stick figure."

We stopped to look up at the sky. An ominous patch of dark gray clouds was moving overhead.

"The clouds are following us."

"It's going to rain any minute now."

The leaves were blowing up off the sidewalk.

"Rain, rain, go away . . ." I started to sing.

"Claudia and I are here to say . . ." Erica responded.

"Please come back another day!" we shouted out together.

It grew dark so fast. We reached the Pikes' house just as a clap of thunder pealed and a few fat raindrops fell on our heads.

As Mrs. Pike answered the door, the sky opened up.

"Hurry, girls, and get in out of that rain."

Erica introduced herself to Mrs. Pike.

"I'm so glad you could make it on such short notice. I'll only be gone for a couple of hours." Mrs. Pike was clearly exasperated. "I have to bring Vanessa to an emergency rehearsal at her ballet class. She has a recital the day before Thanksgiving and we still don't have her outfit."

I promised Mrs. Pike we'd make sure the triplets did their homework. Nicky (who's eight) and Margo (who's seven) were at the computer. Five-year-old Claire was watching a cartoon video. We were lucky. Only six kids to watch today, not seven.

"Everyone into the living room," I called out after we waved good-bye to Mrs. Pike and Vanessa. "Guys, this is Erica Blumberg, and she and I are sitting for you today."

Jordan, one of the ten-year-old triplets, said something under his breath and snickered.

Byron, another triplet, punched him on the arm. "Cut it out, Jordan, or Mom is going to — "

Jordan punched him back . . .

. . . and I separated them.

Claire and Margo had moved to the sofa, hands folded in their laps.

"Hello," they said simultaneously.

Erica asked if they wanted to play a game and they said, "Yesss!"

I went into the kitchen to get a glass of water. When I came back, I saw Jordan sitting on the edge of the sofa, staring down Byron. Adam was laughing hysterically.

"Claudia, help me. He won't cut it out," Byron exclaimed. "Stop staring! It's giving me the jeebies!" (Byron has become the most serious of the triplets.)

"Get upstairs and do your homework, boys, before I count to ten — or else," I threatened, looming over Jordan's head.

Jordan glared up at me. "You ruin everything, Claudia."

"One . . . two . . . three . . ."

"You can't tell me what to do," Jordan said.

"Four . . . five . . ."

"Me neither," Adam, the third triplet, joined in.

"It's a free country. I can do whatever I want."

"Six . . . seven . . ."

"Me too."

"Eight . . . nine . . ."

But by the time I got to ten, the boys sped upstairs, taking two steps at a time.

Erica watched them in amazement.

When the triplets were quiet, I decided to check on Nicky, and Erica returned to her game with the girls.

Suddenly, we heard a crash.

Something had smashed on the floor directly over our heads.

"What's above us?" Erica asked with a look of concern. "I hope it isn't Mr. and Mrs. Pike's room."

"No — Jordan and Adam's room." I groaned. Then we marched upstairs.

"Jordan and Adam Pike, come here this instant!" I called from the top of the stairs. "Right now!"

No response.

"Adam? Jordan?" I knocked three times on their bedroom door. "I know you two are in there. Open up."

From behind the door Jordan squeaked, "Are you sure you want us to open up?"

"Yes, we're sure. Open the door."

"Are you absolutely, abso-toot-ly sure?"

"Yes," Erica and I said together.

"Okay, you asked for it."

Jordan threw open the door and Frodo (the Pikes' pet hamster) darted into the hall.

Erica screeched and leaped onto a bench.

Jordan and Adam flew out of the room after Frodo.

I burst into laughter.

As usual, disaster at the Pike house had erupted in full force. It was like a volcano. Once it started to explode, you couldn't stop the lava.

"It's a RAT!" Erica screamed. Byron peeked out of the room he shares with Nicky, then closed the door firmly.

I laughed harder.

"R-r-rat. Big. Brown. Fluffy!"

"Fluffy?" I was laughing even harder than before. "Erica, that was Frodo."

"Frodo?! Who's Frodo?!"

"The Pikes' hamster. Jordan and Adam were probably playing and knocked over his cage."

I pushed their bedroom door all the way open.

"It's worse than I thought. Erica, welcome to the baby-sitting job guaranteed to drive you batty."

"Batty or *ratty*?" Erica snorted and jumped off the bench. "Claudia, in case you hadn't noticed, I'm not very comfortable with the idea of a mouse in the house."

Jordan reappeared with a squirming and wiggling Frodo in his hands.

I pointed to the mess and sucked in my laughter. Time to be serious.

"What exactly happened?" I asked him and Adam, eyes on the collapsed hamster cage. The floor was a mess of sawdust, hamster pellets, and plastic pieces.

Jordan was suddenly very quiet. He handed Frodo to Adam.

That's when Erica stepped in. She flashed Jordan a sinister look. "Speechless, hmmm? Well, then, there is only one thing we can do in this situation," she whispered, edging closer and closer to him.

And then she did it.

She tickled Jordan.

"Stop stop stop pleeeeeease!" He screeched.

She'd found his weak spot. After only twenty minutes of baby-sitting, Erica Blumberg had conquered Jordan Pike. I was impressed.

Jordan was begging for mercy.

"So, Jordan, are you ready to give up?"

"I give! I give! I give up!"

Erica stopped tickling.

"Ordanjay! At'swhay appeninghay?" Adam spoke up.

Byron shouted from his own room. "Ordanjay, ooklay athay ouyay!"

Jordan looked defeated, but he yelled back. "Ickquay! Et'slay akemay ahay unray orfay itthay!"

That was their last-ditch escape effort: pig latin.

But the amazing Erica was on to this trick too.

"Make a run for it, Jordan? I happen to be fluent in pig latin, and I understood everything you said."

Now Jordan was *really* defeated.

Adam and Byron were crushed too.

Erica had won.

I couldn't believe I had worried about whether she would be a good baby-sitter. She was awesome. She had the triplets under control in minutes. Except for the hamster mess, it was a job well done.

We marched the boys into Adam and Jordan's

room and began picking up and reassembling Frodo's red plastic Habitrail set.

I wished I had had a camera that afternoon. It was quite a sight. The Pike triplets (who swore they despised baby-sitters) were suddenly listening, behaving, and *cleaning*.

I think Jordan had a crush on Erica. She could have asked him to do anything and he would have done it.

As we cleared away the last of the mess, Erica caught my eye.

"Hey, Claudia, it's getting kind of late. What time is it now?"

"What time is it?" I knew what she wanted me to say and so I played along. "Uh, gee, Erica, I think it's time for homework."

The triplets made a lot of noise about that, but reluctantly they grabbed their backpacks and opened their textbooks.

The house became very quiet.

"That was great," I said to Erica.

"Yeah, we make a super team, don't you think?"

I was not stressed out about Stacey and Jeremy. For the first time in hours — in days, in weeks — I felt like my old self again. I felt so comfortable with Erica.

"So, do you have a boyfriend?" I asked her while we were tidying up the living room.

Erica chuckled to herself. "Not! I wish."

"Well, Jordan Pike is in love with you." I laughed.

"Very funny."

"Hey, Erica, do you ever get dressed up or wear makeup?"

"Nah. I'm not into that stuff. It makes me feel weird."

I eyed Erica up and down. The wheels in my head were turning.

I suddenly wanted to give Erica a makeover.

I'd start with a ribbon in her hair, then add a matching sweatshirt and a funky pair of sneakers. We could go shopping for stuff together.

"You know, Stacey and I always have a blast when we go shopping and try on clothes."

"Really? Not me."

"Yeah, Stacey and I go shopping together *all the time*." I paused and corrected myself. "Or at least we *did* go shopping together all the time."

"Are you guys having a fight or something?" Erica asked.

"You could say that."

In my mind I saw Stacey and Jeremy snuggling at the movies.

Erica put her hand on my shoulder. "Are you okay, Claudia?"

"I guess."

"What happened between you guys?"

That's when I decided to tell Erica the truth, the whole truth, and nothing but the truth.

"Okay. It started with this new kid at school, Jeremy Rudolph. I met him first. I liked him first. I even dated him first . . . but Stacey's got him."

"How does she have him?"

"Well, this may sound mean, but the truth is, she stole him. We had this huge fight about it and now we don't talk anymore. I just can't."

"Wow."

"Is that wrong of me?"

"No way! I can't believe that happened. When she knew you liked this guy and she . . ." Erica shook her head. "Unbelievable."

She wrapped her arm around me.

"It hurts just to think about it."

"Well, you have every right to be mad at her. I would be mad!"

"You would?"

"I would never, ever steal my friend's boyfriend or crush or anything — no matter what. You don't do that to a friend. It's not worth it."

I started to cry.

For the first time in weeks I felt I had someone I could really talk to. Erica wasn't close to Stacey, like Kristy or Mary Anne. She was a great listener. She gave great advice.

And she liked me. She really liked me.

Had I found a new friend?

❋ Chapter 4

The next day I didn't oversleep (thank goodness).
I decided it was time to start over.
I had a new friend. I needed a new attitude.
Oh, and I needed a new look.

I pulled on my favorite red woolen sweater, the one my grandmother Mimi had knitted for me a few years ago, before she died. It looked great when I matched it up with my navy blue skirt, the one with the embroidered flowers along the bottom.

Then I slipped on my favorite platform loafers. I stared in the mirror. Moment of truth. Time to fix my hair.

I thought hard. What would make the biggest statement? I decided at last to wear one braid on each side. I'd seen in a fashion magazine that braids were stylish again.

But, of course, Janine didn't think I was stylish.

"Hey, Pippi Longstocking!" she said when I walked into the kitchen for breakfast.

I ignored her and poured myself a huge bowl of Oat Crunchies. As if Janine were one to talk, sitting there in her boring outfit with her boring haircut.

"I think Claudia looks pretty," my mom said, winking at me. "Red is a good color on you, honey. Isn't that Mimi's sweater?"

I nodded.

"Well, you still look like Pippi to me. Or even better — Pippi gone hippie." Janine laughed at her own joke.

"Pippi Longstocking was a very motivated young woman," Mom said, winking again in my direction. "She was a bold adventurer. She was strong. She had real spirit."

I glanced at the clock. Seven forty-five. I had to hurry if I was going to make it to homeroom on time.

" 'Bye, Mom. Thanks," I said, leaving the house in a whirlwind.

"I love you, my dear," she whispered in my ear as she hugged me. "But please do me a favor. Don't trip in those shoes, okay?" She shut the door behind me and I was off.

When I arrived at SMS, I was determined that today would be the best day I had had in a long time.

I turned and scanned the school grounds on my way through the front entrance. I was searching for Erica.

I had found a friend who accepted me for who I am. This was the beginning of something wonderful. I knew it.

No Erica in the SMS lobby. Mary Anne was standing by the school secretary's office (I waved), but no Erica.

I wandered into the library. No Erica.

Finally, I clomped up to the lockers (the shoes were great, but they did make a lot of noise on the stairs). No Erica there either.

I ducked into the girls' room to check my braids. Looking good. Feeling good. I turned to leave.

I pushed open the bathroom door and —

Wham! Slammed into someone walking by.

Jeremy.

"Hey, Claudia," he said, rubbing his arm.

"Oh, no! I can't believe that just happened."

What I really couldn't believe was that I was standing in the hall at school talking to Jeremy Rudolph. After more than a month. And Stacey was nowhere to be seen.

The first thing I thought was: *I am so embarrassed*.

The second thing I thought was: *Get me out of here*.

The third thing I thought was: *He is so cute*.

Stop thinking, Claudia. It's dangerous.

Jeremy was wearing a long-sleeved rugby shirt and faded jeans. He was perfect. His shaggy sandy brown hair was adorable. Brown eyes. Staring into my eyes.

"Gee. Um. Hi." My voice trembled.

Oh, that was brilliant, Claudia.

"Are you going to your locker?" Jeremy asked. "I'll walk with you."

All around us, kids rushed to and from their lockers, getting ready for first period. But here, next to Jeremy, everything was in slow motion.

S-l-o-o-o-o-o-w   m-o-o-o-o-t-i-o-n.

He was asking me questions, but no answers came out of my mouth. He must have thought I was too shy to say anything. But he kept walking along with me.

Jeremy remembered where my locker was. I was surprised.

"Are your classes going well?" he asked me.

I smiled. But still no words came out.

By this time, he must have decided I was giving him the silent treatment.

The truth is, I felt like I had a frog in my throat and rocks in my head. I shifted from one foot to the other. I was pathetic. I couldn't look him straight in the eye.

"I have so much homework," he continued, still trying to start up a conversation. He was shifting from foot to foot too. Nervous?

"Oh?" I sounded ridiculous. *Oh?*

I was unable to form complete sentences.

He looked so cute.

Stop that. What was I thinking? Stacey was Jeremy's girlfriend. Not me. He'd made his choice. And his choice was Stacey McGill.

"Yeah, I have so much homework. Do you?" he asked.

"Homework?" I repeated.

"Yeah."

I made a doofy face and smiled.

"Yeah, well, I'm pretty excited about Thanksgiving," Jeremy continued, leaning on my locker while I got my books together. "Time off and all that. Are you excited?"

What was he still doing here? Why was he still talking to me?

Act cool, Claudia. Aloof. I didn't want him to get the wrong idea.

"Actually, I'm super-psyched because my Thanksgiving is going to be totally different this year," Jeremy said.

"Different?"

I looked into his eyes. Could he read my mind? *Jeremy Rudolph* (my thoughts transmitted a secret message), *are you trying to tell me something?*

"Yeah. This year I might ask Stacey to come over. I'm a little nervous about that."

Wham!

Stacey?

I smiled politely and pulled out my purple notebook and my tattered copy of *Wuthering Heights,* which we were reading in class.

Heathcliff and Cathy. Jeremy and Claudia.

Two couples. Both doomed from the start.

"I have to go to class," I said and glanced away.

"Look, Claudia." Jeremy touched my arm. "I really do want to be friends with you. I miss not talking to you like this."

I looked up. "You do?"

"Well, you know what I mean." He smiled down at me. "Plus, I've been meaning to ask, are you and Stacey not speaking because of me?"

"No, well . . . that's not — "

"Claudia, I don't know that many people in Stoneybrook and the last thing I want to do is lose one of the few friends I do have. Like you."

I felt a little flushed. *Was I blushing?*

"It isn't your fault," I blurted out. "It isn't your fault at all."

He sighed. "Can we be friends, please?"

I nodded. "How's your arm? I really whacked you with that door. I'm the one who should be apologizing."

"Well, the swelling will go down eventually."

"You know, Jeremy, I think the thing with Stacey was bound to happen."

"But you two seemed so close."

"We were. We were best friends for life. Or at least I thought so. But I guess some things change." I closed my locker door.

"Well, maybe I can say something that will help the two of you — " Jeremy began, hope in his eyes.

"Don't," I mumbled, twisting one of my braids with my fingers.

"Your hair looks cool, by the way."

He liked my braids.

"So," he continued, "now that you're speaking to me, what *are* you up to for Thanksgiving?"

"My family's having a big turkey dinner. No real surprises. Except that my aunt's friend is coming . . ."

Suddenly, we were having a normal conversation. About normal things. Like family and friends. I told Jeremy about the day my cousin, Lynn, was born and how my aunt had taken my middle name for the baby. We talked for a few minutes about babies, and I even pulled out a picture of Lynn that I'd stuck inside my notebook. Jeremy had cousins who lived in Boulder, Colorado.

The homeroom bell rang.

"Wow, is it already — ?" I checked my watch.

"Yeah, time sure flies when you're . . ."

Uh-oh.

I gazed down the hall.

Just over Jeremy's shoulder I saw . . .

Stacey. Glaring at us.

I took a giant step backward, away from my locker and away from Jeremy.

"So, I'll see you around, then?"

"Hey, what's up? Why are you running off?" Jeremy asked.

I tilted my head in Stacey's direction. "I think maybe you better go too. Someone's waiting."

He turned and saw Stacey. "Oh."

"Later, Jeremy."

"Yeah. Later. See you around."

"See you around." And, after a beat, I called out, "Thanks again!"

Jeremy turned back to me and smiled a big, warm, friendly smile. Then he walked over to Stacey (who was still glaring at us), and she tossed her head back and snaked her arm around his waist.

That was her way of saying, *Hands off, Claudia. He's mine.*

But he'd been so nice.

I was more confused than ever.

❋ Chapter 5

"So tell me again what happened," my aunt Peaches said as we cleared away the dinner dishes that night.

Mom and Janine were in Peaches' living room with Lynn and my uncle Russ, while Peaches and I launched a Kishi gabfest in the kitchen. My dad was coming to pick us up later, after an evening business meeting in Stamford.

"Okay." I started to talk quickly as I wiped off the kitchen table. "First, I liked Jeremy. But I found out Jeremy liked Stacey. Now I think Jeremy likes me again. But Stacey doesn't like me and I don't like her. And I don't know what else."

Peaches' mouth dropped open and she looked at me with an exaggerated stare. "Huh?"

"I know, I know. It's like a soap opera."

Peaches nodded.

"I'm just confused. What should I do?"

"Maybe you're thinking about it too much."

"Why are you always right, Peaches?"

"Practice, practice, practice."

I started to ask Peaches another question, but Janine waltzed into the kitchen with Lynn. The baby was quietly sucking on a blanket on Janine's shoulder, looking even more adorable than usual. Of course, her outfit may have had something to do with that.

Lynn wore a blue romper with teeny yellow stars on it, an intergalactic outfit contributed by yours truly, Godmother Claudia. I had made it for Lynn the month before. I dyed a plain white romper indigo, then decorated it with a bright yellow, nontoxic, washable paint pen. (I got the idea from a clothing craft book Mom had borrowed from the library.)

Whenever I saw Lynn, Peaches always dressed her in the artsy outfits I'd made. I thought it was special that she remembered to do that for me. She always magically knew what it took to make me feel better about myself.

Janine cooed at the baby and I tugged gently on Lynn's toes.

The doorbell rang. It was Dad.

"Hello, hello, Kishis!" Dad said as he entered the kitchen.

"Hello, hello, Dad."

I wished everyone would leave the kitchen so Peaches and I could finish our talk.

The kettle whistled. "Tea's on!" Peaches said. She poured Dad a steaming cup of Darjeeling.

"Where's your mother?" Dad asked Janine.

"Upstairs with Russ."

"Okay." Dad left with his tea.

"Janine, would you mind changing the baby for me?" my aunt asked politely.

"Sure." Janine left with Lynn.

"Now, where were we before we were interrupted, Claudia?" Peaches smiled. Sometimes she can read my mind. "Oh, I know. I wanted to tell you something. You know my best friend, Molly, is coming to visit next week, right? Well, believe it or not, I haven't seen her in two years."

"Two whole years?" I thought about what it would be like if I didn't see one of my friends for two years. It seemed like forever.

"We were best pals in college. She called a couple of weeks ago, out of the blue. In a moment of craziness, I invited her for Thanksgiving dinner."

"Wow. You must really miss her."

"I do. She's been traveling the world for a few years. She's a photojournalist, an excellent one. She takes pictures for national newspapers and news-magazines."

I was impressed. I didn't know Aunt Peaches knew someone who traveled all over the world. Someone who took pictures for *Time* and *Newsweek*.

"Do you write or talk on the phone to each other?" I asked. "When do you have time to catch up?"

"Oh, we don't always have time to catch up. In fact, we're both pretty lousy at keeping in touch. We try, but sometimes life just takes over. It's funny, but even though we're great old friends, Molly and I are opposites."

"What do you mean?" I asked.

"In college, we disagreed about everything. She'd want to go to the library. I'd want to go dancing. We didn't like the same kind of movies, but we always went together anyway. Go figure."

"Sounds like you weren't really meant to be friends."

"No, no. We were *definitely* meant to be friends. If I ever needed Molly for anything really important, she was there for me. I remember this one time . . ."

Peaches' voice trailed off. "Oh, you don't care about these silly stories."

"Of course I do. Tell me what happened."

"Well, one time in college Molly and I were invited to this fabulous party on campus. We were thrilled and we planned for *weeks*. Our dresses, our hair, our shoes. We wanted everything to be just right. The only trouble was, well, I had a HUGE crush on this boy, Billy Bradford. But I was too afraid to admit it to anyone, even Molly." Peaches rolled her eyes. "And I knew he was also going to be at that party."

"So what happened?"

"So finally it was the night of the party. Naturally, it started badly. First, Molly and I got locked out of our dormitory. We waited almost an hour before someone from campus security came to let us in. Then it started to pour. We were more than two hours late for the party."

"What a nightmare!"

"And by the time we finally did arrive, soaked to the skin, everyone was staring at us. Oh it was just *awful*. But believe it or not, the worst was yet to come. The minute we walked in, you'll never guess who strolled over to Molly."

"Not — "

"Yes! Billy Bradford. Molly was beaming . . . and I was fuming. And he didn't leave her side for the entire party. Danced only with her. Talked only with her. I don't even think he remembered my name." Peaches shook her head. "I was utterly destroyed. I practically spent the entire party in the bathroom while my best friend laughed and danced cheek-to-cheek with *my* boy."

Peaches laughed. But I didn't think it was funny. How could Molly do that to my aunt?

"The thing was, Molly didn't do anything on purpose," Peaches continued. "She didn't know about my crush until the next day, when I confronted her."

"And then she apologized and let you go out with him, right?" I said hopefully.

"Wrong." My aunt made a noise like a buzzer on a quiz show. "By then it was too late. Molly liked him and he liked her and she was not willing to give him up. Of course, we had a giant fight about it. We said all sorts of mean things. I accused her of stealing my boyfriend. . . ."

That sounded familiar.

"We argued for days, weeks, even. Once we had a yelling match in the library and were so noisy that this student librarian guy threatened to throw us out.

Then Molly stormed off and I was left standing with the guy, crying hysterically."

"Were you embarrassed? Did you get thrown out?"

"No. Not when I started crying. The librarian actually *took* me out. For a cup of coffee."

"That was nice. I guess."

"That cup of coffee changed my life."

"It did? How?"

"Claudia, the student librarian was Russ."

I was dumbfounded. "Russ?"

"Yes indeed. So you see," Peaches continued, "if Molly hadn't made me cry, I never would have met your uncle in the library that night. At least that's how I see it. Sometimes your emotions get the best of you. And funny things happen along the way. Things happen for a reason."

My aunt and uncle had met because Molly and Peaches had had a fight in the middle of the library? Wow.

"That's some story," I said.

Peaches brushed her hand against my cheek.

"The thing about fights with friends, Claudia, is that they don't usually last forever. You and Stacey will figure this one out. Trust me. Just like Molly and I did."

I wanted to believe that — desperately.

"Claudia, maybe you should think about giving Stacey a call. To talk things over."

I wasn't sure.

"Peaches, do you think that Stacey and I are friends like you and Molly are friends?"

Peaches took my hand. "Claudia, your friendship with Stacey is unique. I'm afraid the only people who can solve your problem are you and Stacey."

On the way home, I thought about calling Stacey to talk things over.

Maybe it was my responsibility to make the first move.

If I apologized first, it *would* take the pressure off. I wouldn't have to feel awkward at school. The BSC meetings would be back to normal. Kristy would certainly be happy.

So it was decided.

I would call Stacey.

Walking into my room, I checked the answering machine.

Two red blinks. Two messages.

Maybe one was from Stacey. Wouldn't that be great?

Beep.

It was Mrs. Pike. She was happy to hear about

the new sitter, Erica Blumberg. Apparently, Jordan wanted to know when Erica was coming back again.

Zzzzzzzzzt. I fast-forwarded to the next message.

Beep.

"Hey, Claudia, it's Mrs. Pike again. Just want to know if you and Erica can be here Monday at three-thirty for another job."

I hit ERASE. I'd call her the next day about the details.

I stretched out on my bed and flipped through an art catalog, making a mental note to stop by the Artist's Exchange over the weekend. I needed materials for the centerpiece I was going to make for our Thanksgiving dinner.

I glanced at the phone. *Should I call Stacey?*

I read the catalog. *Nah.*

I stared at the phone. *Yes. Definitely.*

I flipped the catalog pages again. *Nope.* Too uncomfortable.

I glared at the phone. *Okay. Okay. I would do it.*

But just as I was about to dial her number, I had a change of heart.

I could NOT call Stacey McGill.

I listened to a little voice inside my head.

What about all those mean things Stacey said the

last time you spoke? She said you weren't a real friend or a real artist.

That hurt.

Why should I call Stacey before she called me?

I'd call Erica instead.

✸ Chapter 6

This morning, on the corner of Bradford Court, I saw a black cat. You know what that means.

Bad luck.

Ever since my fight with Stacey, I'd felt cursed. A black cloud followed me wherever I went.

Now a black cat was following me too.

Coincidence?

I didn't think so.

No wonder Jeremy didn't like me. No wonder I'd broken up with my best friend in the whole world. I was cursed.

"Hey, Claudia, nice hat!" Kristy saw me on my way into Stoneybrook Middle School. She was running pretty fast so we didn't stop to talk.

Oh, well. Even with a curse on me, I could still be fashionable. That was something, I guess. No one had to know that the reason I was wearing my floppy brown felt hat was to hide myself from the rest of the world.

I moved slowly upstairs toward the lockers. At the top, I pushed through a group of seventh-graders and walked into . . .

Jeremy Rudolph.

"Cool hat!" he said.

On the way to second period, I stopped in the hall to take a drink from the fountain.

Jeremy was there too.

Coincidence?

Hmmm.

"Hello again," I said.

"Yeah, hey," he replied, smiling. His teeth were very white. Like vanilla ice cream.

I checked around to make sure Stacey wasn't standing nearby. (That would be my bad luck creeping up.)

But she wasn't.

I went to math class feeling a little better. Two Jeremy sightings in one morning.

After math, on the way to third-period science, I was beginning to think there was a conspiracy at Stoneybrook Middle School.

There he was *again*.

I called out, "Jeremy?" as he was walking past the lab.

He slapped his forehead and said, "Claudia? We have to stop meeting like this." Then he moved down the hall toward his own science room.

By the time lunch rolled around, I was actually thinking that maybe today would end up being a good one.

But a voice inside my head interrupted.

Not so fast.

I decided to avoid crowds and took a shortcut to the cafeteria. That way I wouldn't have to see anyone.

There's a passageway next to the gym that only teachers and janitors at Stoneybrook use. My art teacher had spilled the beans once and pointed it out. I knew I wasn't the only kid who used it, but since it was so off the beaten track, I hadn't seen many people down there.

And there I was, walking along, minding my own business, when all of a sudden . . . Jeremy Rudolph was walking toward me.

"This is too much!" I exclaimed. "Are you following me?"

"I was going to ask you the same question," Jeremy said. But he seemed uncomfortable.

"Is someone trying to tell us something?" I joked.

"Uh, no . . . well . . . I don't know what you mean." Jeremy turned to look behind him and then turned back quickly. That's when I heard *her* turn the corner.

"Jeremy, wait up! I want to show you some — "

Stacey. She swallowed the rest of her sentence.

"Oh, hello, Claudia." She gripped Jeremy's arm.

"Hello, Stacey." My body felt like lead. I couldn't move forward or backward. (*I* didn't have someone to hold on to.)

Jeremy was squirming.

Suddenly they turned to walk away.

"Well, have a nice lunch," Stacey said, smirking as they headed to the cafeteria together, leaving me alone in the corridor.

Jeremy gave me an awkward shrug.

I followed them from a safe distance and made my way into the lunchroom — alone.

What had just happened?

DELUXE LASAGNA. PEAS. SWEDISH MEATBALLS.

The hot-lunch special didn't sound too bad.

But it looked disgusting.

It was the salad bar for me.

I scanned the room for familiar faces but quickly

realized that finding a seat in the lunchroom today would be difficult.

It used to be so easy. The BSC members always sat together at the same table. We'd gab, eat, and gossip.

Those were the days. Now it seemed like our problems with school or teachers or other kids didn't even compare to our own problems. It wasn't us against them anymore. It was us against *us*.

I peeked at the salad fixings. Out of the corner of my eye, I saw where Stacey and Jeremy had taken their seats. She was talking and he was listening. Or at least he was pretending to listen. He didn't look very interested from where I was watching. Or maybe I just wished that were true. After all, he wouldn't have been sitting there if he didn't like her.

I moved over to the dessert table and scanned the selections. A few seconds later, just as I glanced over to see how things were going with Stacey and Jeremy, Rachel Griffin sat down at their table.

Rachel Griffin? Now, that was interesting. What were they talking about over there? Rachel used to be a major pain in the neck, very clingy but always acting superior. She moved to London with her parents a few years ago and most of us lost touch with her. But recently the Griffins returned to Stoney-brook, and Rachel came back to SMS.

Whatever.

I wasn't planning on hanging out with her anytime soon.

I looked off in the direction of the BSC table. Kristy and Mary Anne were there with Abby (who I hadn't seen in awhile). But they didn't notice me, so I didn't call out to them.

For the first time in a long time, I didn't know where I fit in.

I was about to sit down at a table by myself (which is a last resort, believe me), when I saw a familiar face on the other side of the room. Erica was waving to me. I hurried to sit with my new friend.

"Another great outfit, Claudia," she said as I slipped into my seat.

I took an enormous bite of a cookie.

"Nutrition will get you everywhere," she teased.

"I pick chocolate chips over lettuce any day of the week," I said. I grinned.

Somehow, I suddenly felt that everything was okay in the world . . . sitting here with Erica instead of with my BSC friends or Jeremy. I felt it in my bones.

Erica and I traded stories about the day so far.

Her class had begun dissecting frogs in science lab, and she said that some boy had puked on the lab table.

"That guy over there," she said, pointing to Wellner Wallace. "What a geek. I think it was the formaldehyde smell that got to him, actually."

I turned to look at Wellner but caught another glimpse of Stacey and Jeremy instead. And Stacey wasn't talking. She was staring. At Erica and me.

Hmmm. Maybe *she* was jealous for a change. Stacey wasn't the only one with a new friend.

We chatted and ate, then suddenly I had a brilliant idea.

"Hey, Erica, want to go shopping this weekend?"

"Shopping? Well, I'm not really much of a shopper."

"But it's almost the holidays. A weekend trip to the mall is essential."

"Well, okay, I guess so. But I'll only go shopping under one condition."

"What? Anything!"

"No expectations. I'm not the easiest shopper in the galaxy. So I'm apologizing in advance, okay?"

"Don't apologize. It'll be great! We can go to Artist's Exchange. I need some materials for a centerpiece I'm making. I'm building a scene of the first Thanksgiving table."

"Sounds historical."

Brrrrrrrrrrrrrrang!

The first lunch bell rang, so we walked to the kitchen to turn in our trays and plates.

"I'll call you tonight, Claudia, okay?"

Erica went off to study hall and I headed toward my locker.

If someone had taken a Polaroid photo of me then, he or she would have captured a look of happiness. I was going to the Washington Mall with my new friend. Things were looking up. No more bad omens. The Kishi curse had been lifted.

Brrrrrrrriiiiiiing!

The second lunch bell rang — and I was running late.

I shoved the next period's books into my backpack, slammed my locker, and whirled around. There was Stacey. She ignored me.

Weird.

And there was Jeremy . . . where else? Behind her.

He raised his eyebrows.

"What can I say?" he said. "Hello *again*."

As I watched them walk away, Jeremy turned back to glance at me.

Stacey didn't see him do *that*.

✳ Chapter 7

"What are you wearing?" Janine sniffled and coughed. "It looks like you did your hair in the dark."

Janine always knows just the right thing to say.

She was commenting on my new hairdo (little ponytails all over my head — I saw it in a magazine) and my oversized angora sweater, which I'd purchased with Mom at a tag sale in the neighborhood. It was blue and furry and I loved it. Mom said it was from the fifties.

Sometimes I let Janine's comments bother me, but today she wasn't going to make me feel bad.

I, Claudia Kishi, was on my way to an excellent mall excursion. And I was, of course, wearing an excellent mall outfit. I wondered what Erica was planning to wear.

I haven't always loved shopping this much. Not until I met Stacey. She and I used to go to the mall together all the time. But now that Stacey and I weren't going anywhere together, it felt great to have another friend to do things with.

I told Erica to meet me at the fountain in the center of the mall. It's the perfect meeting spot. And there's this incredible pink water (I think it's a lighting trick) that shoots up into the air.

I arrived a little late, but Erica was perched on a bench, waiting.

She grinned when she saw me and my sweater and my hairdo.

"Claudia Lynn Kishi, the fashion queen!"

"Hello!" I said, laughing, and pulled her off the bench. We had things to do, people to see, places to go.

First stop: Flashbox. Official home of punk clothes and trendy things. It sounds a little "out there," but it isn't at all. Besides, Stacey shops there all the time. This summer they added a whole section devoted to affordable (and cool) jewelry. I just *had to* check it out with Erica. A promising fashion queen needed just the right jewelry, I announced.

"But I really don't wear jewelry, Claudia," Erica moaned as I led her to a wall of earrings.

Flashbox has everything wild you could ever want to wear. Stacey once bought sparkly lens-less glasses. They sell mood rings, wire bracelets, giant hair clips, daisy barrettes, little mesh bags, fake leopard purses, and removable tattoos.

Erica wandered around one of the spinning carousels with anklets and chokers hanging on it. I pulled off a necklace for her. It was made from colored beads that spelled out PEACE. Stacey would have loved a necklace like this.

"I don't really like this kind of jewelry, Claudia," Erica told me. "I definitely don't want to wear a word around my neck."

What about making a statement? Obviously, no one had ever shown Erica the simple joys of shopping for accessories. That's where I came in. I had a responsibility.

"How about these?" I asked, holding up a pair of plain silver hoops.

She shook her head no.

"Moonstones?" I asked, holding up another, simpler beaded necklace.

She shook her head again.

"Then what, Erica? Hair combs?"

"I have short hair, Claudia."

I crossed to a shelf on one side of the store and

reached for a diary/datebook that was marked down. It was covered with blue furry material.

"How about this?" I asked. "You don't have to wear it, but it's fun."

Erica laughed. "Ha! Claudia, it matches your sweater!"

She was right. Hmmm. I had to keep searching for something that would be right for Erica and only for Erica.

"Claud, let's go somewhere else," Erica said softly, and headed for the exit.

I bounded after her. "Okay! How about Macy's?"

"Too many people. Department stores make me nauseous."

"Nauseous? Okay, then let's go to Artist's Exchange. It'll be nice and quiet."

An elevator at the Washington Mall is like an amusement park ride. It's glass enclosed so you can see everything on the way up and down. We got on with a mother and her little boy, who kept pressing his nose to the glass and squealing.

"This place is like magic," Erica said, pressing her own nose to the glass as well. "They have Christmas decorations up everywhere! And look at all the people. And the stores. Everything is sparkling like they just sprayed a gallon of Windex on the mir-rors."

The doors opened and we moved quickly toward the art supply shop. I pulled out my shopping list and asked the clerk to point me in the direction of crepe paper.

While I debated for a long five minutes about which shade of orange crepe paper I wanted to pur-chase, Erica collected a bunch of items she thought I might like for the centerpiece.

First she handed me a tube of gold glitter glue and a package of different-colored feathers. "Claudia, you can make a disco turkey with these. It can dance to rock and roll music. How about some *Plymouth* rock and roll?"

"Ha-ha-ha." I pretended to be disgusted with her goofy joke, but I was laughing.

She passed me a pack of colored foil papers and an origami kit.

"Hey, since your family is Japanese, why not make origami turkeys?"

What a cool idea, I thought, reading the direc-tions on the origami package. It sounded a little chal-lenging, but I'd give it a try. I could fold small birds for everyone's place setting.

Wow. When we were in Flashbox, Erica seemed

so uninterested in anything I had to say or wanted to show her. But now, in the art supply shop, she was darting around, grabbing objects and putting them together in combinations that really worked — artistically speaking, that is. I'd had no idea that Erica was so creative.

Erica Blumberg was my new *creative* friend.

"Are you hungry?" I asked as we paid for the paper and glitter and walked out into the mall again. "Want to hit the food court?"

"Mmmmmmn. D'oh-nuts!" she said, grunting in her finest Homer Simpson imitation.

I jumped in with my impression. "Mmmmmn. Tah-cos. D'oh!"

We agreed that Mexican food sounded the yummiest, so we headed for Tortilla Queen.

Erica ordered a taco and a large diet Coke. I ordered a taco too, with extra, extra cheese, and a grape soda.

"Oh, before I forget to tell you!" I said when we were seated. "Mrs. Pike called to ask if we would baby-sit again this Monday. It seems that Jordan has developed a little bit of a crush on — "

Erica interrupted with, "Little ol' me?"

I chuckled and bit into my taco. "So can you do it?"

"Totally. I loved baby-sitting this week."

"Baby-sitting is soooo much better when you have a partner. That's what Stacey and I've always said."

Erica wiped salsa from the corners of her mouth. "You and Stacey always baby-sat together?"

"A lot. But right now that's just about the last thing in the world I would want to do."

"What's happening with Jeremy and Stacey?"

"Now, that's weird too. I keep running into him at school. Like our paths are meant to cross. I feel funny about it. Isn't that stupid?"

"Why not? Maybe he likes you, Claudia. Maybe Stacey is old news."

"What?"

"Claudia, Jeremy wouldn't talk to you if he wasn't interested in you."

"Yeah, but we're just talking like friends. I mean, he and Stacey are still a couple."

Erica considered this. Then she said, "Well, you and Stacey will make up, I know you will. It'll just take some time."

I leaned on one elbow and sighed. "I actually used to feel that Stacey was more like a sister than a friend. She's more like a sister than my own sister is, anyway. I mean, Janine's not so bad. It's just that Stacey and I had a lot more in common."

I felt that I could tell Erica anything at that moment. There we were, in the middle of the hustle and bustle of Washington Mall, and I was spilling my secrets to someone I had really only just started to know.

But I trusted her.

I asked her if she had any secrets to share too. It was like we were playing truth or dare, without the dare.

She thought for a moment, then nodded. "But it isn't really a secret. . . . I was adopted."

"*Really?*"

Erica was taken aback by my reaction. "You say that like I have some kind of disease or something."

"Oh, noooooooo!" I recovered quickly. "What I mean is . . . Well, if you knew me better . . . See, I had this adoption thing a little while ago. I thought that maybe *I* was adopted . . . and I thought about it all the time. I didn't mean anything *bad* by what I said."

"*Were* you adopted?"

"No. But I imagined it. For two weeks. It's just that I don't look like my sister or anyone else in the family."

"Well, I don't look like anyone in my family either. And I'm grateful, because my brother is a little troll!"

We laughed.

"Erica, when did you find out?"

"I've always known. For as long as I can remember. My parents adopted me right after I was born. I was three weeks old, actually."

"So your parents told you everything about it?"

"They told me a lot. They arranged my adoption through an agency. It was when my parents thought they couldn't have kids."

I nodded.

"But then later my mom got pregnant. My brother is my parents' biological child."

"Do you know who your biological parents are?"

Erica shifted in her seat. "That's where things get sticky."

"Sticky?"

"Lately I've been talking with my mom and dad about searching for my birth parents. Because I *do* want to find out who they are. But Mom and Dad aren't comfortable with that idea."

"How come?"

Erica paused thoughtfully. "Claudia, my parents

let me do whatever I want. They trust me. But right now I think they're trying to protect me. My mom doesn't want me to get hurt or be disappointed by what I find . . . *if* I find anything. Like, what if my birth mother isn't alive? Or what if she doesn't want to see *me*? It's very complicated."

I suddenly admired Erica's strength, curiosity, and determination. I wanted some of that for myself.

"And what does your brother think about all this?" I asked.

"Like I said," Erica responded, "Mike is a troll. But he's only five. He doesn't know the difference between biological or adopted or anything else."

"Why do you want to find your birth parents?" I asked.

"I'm not really sure. It's just something I feel I need to do. I'm curious."

We finished our tacos and sodas. I looked at my watch. It was already two o'clock. If we still wanted to hit a few more stores we had to get a move on.

We began to circle the mall again. Erica stopped short in front of Critters, a pet store. A pair of chocolate Labrador puppies wriggled around in the window. One of them was covered with sawdust.

"Puppies!" Erica said, grinning from ear to ear. "Look at how cuuuuuute they are!"

"Do you like animals?" I asked her.

She nodded. "Definitely."

"Stacey likes animals too. Especially pigs."

"Stacey likes pigs? Well, they are kind of cute, I guess. But puppies are much cuter!"

We walked past the Gap, a coffee bar, a jeweler, and Soundscapes (where I get a lot of my favorite CDs). Then Erica exclaimed, "Look, the Cheese Outlet! Is that all they sell? I bet we'd have a *gouda* time there!"

I giggled. "Be serious! We're here to do *serious* shopping, aren't we?"

"Claudia, I am *brie*-ing serious!"

She was out of control. I loved it.

We ducked into a shoe store, a camping store, and then Old Navy before we finally decided we'd better call Mrs. Blumberg to pick us up.

Walking toward the exit, I noticed a new addition to the video game arcade. They'd installed a photo booth.

"Let's go!" I grabbed Erica's wrist and pulled her into the arcade.

She started to giggle and then I started to giggle and neither of us could stop.

We put eight quarters into the machine and squished into the tiny booth.

"Say *cheese*!" Erica cried.

"Cheese?"

We burst into hysterics. The light flashed.

"Grouchy face!" Erica said, pursing her lips.

Flash!

"Kissy face!"

Flash!

"Friends forever!" Erica said, her arm around my shoulders.

The last light flashed and we were still laughing. Friends forever.

The pictures came out great. In one of them, we were laughing so hard we actually look like we're screaming.

These would definitely be going up in my locker.

❋ Chapter 8

On Sunday morning the sun was shining brightly for the first time all week.

It was a good omen (I hoped).

Erica was a great new friend. We'd had a blast at the mall. She made me laugh harder than I'd laughed in a long time. In fact, I'd laughed so much that I'd forgotten about Stacey and Jeremy.

Well, almost. (You can't expect miracles.)

Erica called me on Sunday morning after breakfast to find out when we were going shopping again.

"You mean you'd actually set foot in Flashbox another time?"

"Well, if you twisted my arm. Who am I to resist fashion counseling from the queen?"

"You'll be wearing blue furry sweaters before you know it."

Erica snorted. "That's what YOU think!"

After I got off the phone with my new best friend, I spent the morning working on my Thanksgiving centerpiece. And I decided to use both of Erica's ideas.

In the center I made a sparkly turkey with the glitter glue, cardboard, and real feathers (not exactly "disco," but it was pretty flashy). I also painted little Styrofoam balls to look like fruit and added leaves cut out of construction paper. Then I wrapped it in a fuzzy velvet bow.

Mom said that she'd get a fat bayberry candle to put in the centerpiece.

"I think it's one of the most creative things you've ever made! Everyone will love it."

I was proud of myself, even if I had strayed from my original design plans.

I also began constructing the teeny origami turkeys for the place settings. However easy they looked to make on the cover of the package, these were tougher than I'd thought.

I ruined about five pieces of foil before I constructed anything that even remotely resembled a bird.

Sigh. The origami would take work. And more time. I'd have to go back to it later.

For now, I was heading over to my aunt's house.

I'd promised Peaches I would stop by to help her get ready for Molly's arrival.

Since Lynn was born, Peaches was always grateful for extra help around the house. And this weekend she was looking for extra, *extra* help so she could make the house perfect.

When I arrived, she looked a bit frazzled. Her hair was twisted up onto her head and she was still wearing her bathrobe, on which there was a wet spot. It looked as if Lynn had spit up.

"Peaches? Are you okay?"

"Oh, Claudia you're here. I'm fine, but Lynn has an upset stomach, Russ had to go to the office for a special breakfast meeting, even though it's *Sunday*, and I have barely started cleaning up."

She collapsed onto a kitchen chair.

The last time I'd seen my aunt so frantic was when she was getting ready to have her baby.

"You look a little tired, Peaches."

"Oh, I shouldn't be complaining. You came over to help me get ready, and that makes all the difference. By the way, let's see your hair today."

I twirled around. Today it was pulled back in five different rainbow barrettes.

"Very colorful, Claudia." My aunt laughed to herself. "I think your being the calm in the middle of my storm is going to do me a world of good."

I glanced at the baby, snuggled into her door swing. Lynn could fall asleep anywhere. Noise didn't bother her. Nothing bothered her. She was the sweetest baby I'd ever seen.

"Okay, kiddo! Time to vacuum." Peaches handed me the vacuum cleaner while she started to dust the windowsill.

Crashhhh!

"My vase! Oh, no!"

Peaches had knocked a glass bud vase off the windowsill. I rushed to help her pick up the broken pieces and mop up the water.

"I am such a klutz this morning."

"What's wrong, Peaches?"

"I'm nervous about Molly. I can't believe she's going to be here tomorrow."

Peaches was worried because she thought Molly would be *bored to death* in Stoneybrook.

After all, she explained to me, Molly had seen the world, met famous people. What in suburban Stoneybrook could possibly compare to that?

"Peaches, Molly doesn't have a baby . . ."

"No, Claudia, you're right. She doesn't." Her face softened. "See, that's why I need you here! Keep telling me that kind of stuff!"

I tried, but my insightful comments didn't take the edge off my aunt's frantic behavior. She continued to clean the house in a fury and wouldn't stop talking about Molly's visit.

"I want everything to be just right. This is a woman who has stayed in the best hotels in the world. I can't let her think my bathroom is a mess, can I?"

My aunt's logic baffled me. If she and Molly were such good friends, what was the difference? If Stacey came into my house and it were messy, I don't think *she'd* mind.

Peaches was walking in circles around the living room, straightening lampshades and fluffing pillows. (I think she refluffed one couch pillow three times.)

Eventually, she went upstairs to straighten up, dragging the vacuum cleaner behind her.

Lynn and I played patty-cake a few times. I built her an awesome castle out of alphabet blocks. I popped a *Wee Sing* video into the VCR.

Upstairs, I could hear the low hum of the vacuum cleaner.

Zzzzzzap!

The power went out.

"Claudia, are you okay?" Peaches yelled from upstairs.

"Yeah. What happened?"

"The vacuum cleaner short-circuited. I'll have to fix it. Aaaaaugh!"

My aunt tore down the stairs, flashlight in hand, rushed to the basement to reset the circuit breaker, and ran upstairs again.

"Do you need any help?" I called out once or twice, but she was in too much of a hurry to answer.

At last the vacuum started again.

When Peaches finally came downstairs, I asked her again what was wrong. "Why are you so nervous?"

"Nervous? Is that what I am?" She sat on the sofa and pulled Lynn into her lap. "I don't know, Claudia. It's more like a mix of nerves and excitement. Friends do that to you sometimes. Do you know what I mean?"

I knew.

"To tell you the truth, Claudia, there's more to it than that. I feel a lot of things. Molly is a big part of my past."

Peaches had thought she would feel relieved to see her long-lost friend. But somewhere deep inside she felt insecure.

Were the old friends too different to get along anymore? Had their lives gone in completely different directions? Had one person's life become much more interesting than the other person's?

"I used to call Molly all the time, but it became too upsetting for me," Peaches confessed. "I put a successful advertising career on hold and opted for the role of stay-at-home mom. Molly became an internationally renowned photographer. I was jealous."

My head was spinning.

Peaches was jealous? *Insecure?* How was that possible? My aunt was the most secure person I knew.

Everything was turned upside down these days. People were acting strangely and nothing was what it seemed to be.

Jeremy, for instance. I had liked him and thought he liked me back.

WRONG.

I believed Stacey would be my very best friend forever.

WRONG.

And I had believed Peaches was one hundred percent secure, happy, fearless. . . .

WRONG.

Why was everyone and everything changing?

Peaches and I moved into the kitchen, where I peeled potatoes and Peaches trimmed green beans for dinner.

"Have you heard anything from Stacey?" she asked me.

I shook my head and shrugged.

"Is she still seeing Jeremy?"

I groaned. "Yes. But I am determined *not* to like him."

Peaches nodded and winked at me. "Of course."

"Did you and Molly ever have another fight?" I asked.

"Believe me, we had more fights. Molly and I shared everything good *and* bad."

"You know, Peaches, I don't think you should worry about what the house looks like or what project you're working on or any of that."

Peaches stopped what she was doing and gave me her complete attention. "Why not?"

For a split second, I had one of those weird out-of-body experiences in which you feel like you're watching yourself. Here I was, a kid, giving advice to a grown-up — and she was really listening.

"Well, you keep saying Molly is so successful. Then why is she alone for Thanksgiving? You're rushing around worrying about her, and she's probably doing the same thing. Why do you feel insecure? What if *she* feels insecure too? You're giving her a family for the holiday."

Peaches looked as if she were about to cry. "A family, Claudia. Right." She hugged me. "I love you." She sighed. "My little niece. Whew. Maybe Molly's visit will turn out just fine. I feel a lot better."

I smiled. "Well, you always make me feel better. It's just my turn to make you feel good."

Lynn gurgled from across the room. I swear she could understand what we were saying.

When I got back home that night, I felt different. Better about myself. After talking to Peaches about Molly, I was more determined than ever to put my situation with Stacey into perspective. I wanted desperately to forget about her and Jeremy. I needed to move on.

Besides, now I had Erica to keep me company.
Rrrrrrring!

I was sure it was Erica calling to tell me about her Sunday skating lessons.

I answered on the third ring. "Hello, Cheese Outlet."

"Uh, Claudia?" It wasn't Erica's voice. "Claudia, is that you?" It wasn't even a girl's voice.

I froze.

"Claudia, it's Jeremy."

❋ Chapter 9

"Jeremy?" I was stunned. He was calling *me*? At home?

My heart was beating like a bongo drum.

Calm down, Claudia. Don't be dramatic.

"Uh, Claudia, are you there?"

"Yes. Of course I'm here. What a surprise!"

"Yeah. So . . . how are you?"

You mean, *besides the fact that I feel flushed all over and my palms are sweating and I feel dizzy?*

"Okay, I guess," I mumbled, desperately trying to conceal my excitement.

"Well, I just wanted to say hi."

"Oh, yeah?"

"Yeah. And to see what was up." He paused. "So what's up?"

"Oh, not much. The sky, the clouds, the birds . . ."

Jeremy chuckled. "But what's up with *you*?"

"Me? Well, I'm making a Thanksgiving turkey out of feathers and glitter. Actually, the floor in my room is covered with glue and paper and it's really a mess right now. It's for a centerpiece."

"That's cool."

I looked at the clock. Eight twenty-four P.M.

What should I say? What should I say? Think fast. Think fast.

"Jeremy, why are you calling me?"

Why did I say that?!

"Uh, well, like I said, I wanted to say hi." Jeremy cleared his throat. "And since we saw each other in school between every period the other day, I figured maybe someone was trying to tell me something."

"Tell you something?"

"Yeah, like we never get a chance to talk in school."

"Oh."

"Am I making any sense?"

"Well . . ."

"So how's school going for you, anyway?" he continued. "You seem so busy."

Okay. That was a question I could deal with. My heart was thumping a little more quietly now.

"Art class? Super. The best."

"Yeah?"

"Yeah. You know, art . . . my whole reason for living . . . the thing that makes me happier than anything else in the entire world."

"Whoa. Yeah, art. I forgot."

He forgot?

"Well, anyway, we're in the middle of making these collages in class and I decided I didn't want mine to be flat like everyone else's so I made a papier-mâché sculpture."

"That's different."

"Yes. Well, I like to be different. Anyway, it's a giant cat, and everything I pasted on it has to do with cats."

"Cat stuff? Like kitty litter?"

"Noooooo." I laughed a little. "Like words and pictures of cats that I drew or cut out of magazines. And other words I like."

"Mm-hmm."

He was pretending to be interested, but I knew what was really going on here. *Change the subject — fast!*

"Sooooo . . . are you getting ready for Thanksgiving?"

"Yeah, well, I think I told you, my family is staying in Stoneybrook," he answered. "We're doing the turkey and cranberry sauce thing. I'll probably watch football with my dad and Gramps."

"Your grandparents are here too?"

"Just Gramps. My grandmother died a couple of years ago."

"Really? Gosh, I'm sorry." I paused. "You know, my grandmother died too. It was so sad. . . ."

"That was your grandmother Mimi, right?"

He remembered her name!

He told me that he hadn't been so close to his Gramma Joan, but he still missed her.

I looked over at my clock again. Eight thirty-six P.M.

Wow. We'd been on the telephone for twelve minutes already. A new world record.

"This is pretty cool, you know that?" Jeremy said.

"What?" I asked.

"Talking on the phone."

Hmmm. If he liked talking on the phone so much, why wasn't he doing it with Stacey?

"Claudia, I said this in school and I meant it. I always wanted to stay friends. I don't want what's happening with me and — "

"Please don't say that," I interrupted him.

"Don't say what?"

"That name. Her name. Whatever."

"Stacey?"

It was still 8:36 P.M. Time had stopped.

Change the subject, Claudia.

"Uh . . . does your family ever go to the movies on Thanksgiving?"

"Uh, sometimes." Jeremy sounded perplexed by my diversion. But he went along with it. "Hey, have you seen *Lovelocked* yet?"

"Actually, I have."

"Me too. I went to see it last weekend with — "

"There she is again!" I interrupted, groaning.

"What? Who? *Stacey?*"

"Yes."

"She *is* my girlfriend, Claudia."

"Yeah, yeah. And you guys went to the movie and held hands and . . ."

"How did you know *that*?" he said.

Oops.

"Jeremy, I was at the same show. Last Saturday. With another friend of mine. You know Mary Anne, right?"

"The same show? Are you sure?"

"I'm sure. I saw you there with Stacey."

Gulp. Did he think I'd been spying on him?

"Oh. Did you like the movie?"

Who was watching the movie? I was watching YOU.

"Mm-hmm." I had a lump in my throat all of a sudden.

"Hey, Claudia, are you going to the science meet?"

Science? Now *he* was changing the subject.

"I'm not exactly what you'd call a science scholar. I'm not a scholar of any kind, come to think of it."

"Why do you say that? You seem really smart."

"Smart? You think so?" I laughed out loud.

"Sure I think so. You're smart and super-creative too. Everyone at SMS likes you."

"You're embarrassing me, Jeremy. Cut it out . . ."

Secretly, I was thinking: *Keep it up, Jeremy.* Who doesn't like compliments?

"Okay. I'm sorry, Claud. I don't want to embarrass you." His voice cracked. "Mrs. Gonzalez says I have a shot at the top science prize. Can you believe that?"

"I bet you'll win the prize. No contest."

"Now you're being nice to me."

Was he flirting with me? Was I flirting with him? We both grew quiet all of a sudden.

"So, what did you do today?" I asked, breaking the silence.

"Skated. I take this class at a rink in Stamford. It's a little bit of a haul but my mom doesn't mind taking me. I want to sign up for Stoneybrook's Junior Hockey League."

"Why don't you just sign up now?" I asked.

"Not good enough yet. And I don't really know anyone in town. I'm kind of shy, in case you hadn't noticed."

"It's hard to notice anything with Stacey always hanging on you."

"Huh?" Jeremy asked. "What did you just say?"

"Uh, forget it. I didn't mean it. It just slipped out."

"Stacey isn't always hanging on me, is she?"

"Well, not always. I didn't mean it that way. It's just that she — "

"I know what this is about. It's you two. Fighting all the time. I know, Stacey talks about it too. You know, maybe I shouldn't have called you up like this. I want to be friends, but if you and Stacey can't work stuff out, I don't want to cause any trouble here."

Stacey talks about it too. I couldn't get that out of my mind. Was she as upset as I was about our "breakup"?

"Claudia, I feel strange talking to you like this. Especially when you and Stacey are having problems. And since I'm going out with her . . ." His voice trailed off.

"What are you trying to say, Jeremy?"

"I mean, if you and Stacey aren't getting along, being friends with both of you just gets in the way."

"Gets in the way of *what*?"

"I guess I'm supposed to be loyal to my girlfriend over a regular friend. And I guess Stacey's my girlfriend . . ."

"Yeah, she is. You keep saying that."

"Anyway, I'm just a little mixed up. Because I really like talking with you too, Claudia."

"Just because Stacey and I are arguing doesn't mean you can't ever talk to me, does it?"

"Yeah, but . . ."

"So maybe sometimes it won't be easy at school."

"Like this week."

"Yeah. At lunch."

"I know you said Stacey grabs me when you're around, and maybe she does, but . . ."

"You don't have to say anything else, Jeremy."

"Yeah, well. I really am okay with it."

Silence.

Fortunately, we overcame that tense moment and talked some more about Thanksgiving (he can't stand stuffing). We also talked about art class (he told me that he loves to draw). We talked about how he felt moving to a new school (he was bummed out because he left a lot of good friends behind in Washington).

We talked about everything *except* Stacey.

I looked over at the clock. Nine twenty-one P.M.

We'd been on the phone for almost an hour.

"Do you realize that it's almost nine-thirty?" I said.

"No way!" he said. "I'll be in trouble if my dad finds out I'm still on the phone. It's so late and it's Sunday! Won't your parents get mad?"

"Well, I have my own phone."

Jeremy sounded impressed. "Wow."

I wasn't about to explain the BSC to him then, so I left it at that.

"So I guess I'll see you around school?" Jeremy joked.

"Around every corner, apparently," I said.

"I'm glad we talked, Claudia."

"Me too. Have a good night."

As I hung up the phone, I heard it again — loud thumping inside my chest. And my mind was racing.

If Stacey knew what had just happened she would —

Better not to think about it.

Stacey didn't have anything to do with Jeremy's calling me. It was his decision and his decision alone. Besides, he just wanted a friend. He was NOT flirting. He was just talking.

Jeremy Rudolph was still dating Stacey McGill. He'd said that.

I reached into my closet to sneak one of the cookies from my secret stash. It was time to eat something sweet.

I, Claudia Kishi, eat whenever I am stressed. And *really*, really confused — like right now.

I wondered if Jeremy felt the same way.

❁ Chapter 10

Never eat Oreo cream filling before bed. You'll wake up with a headache.

That was what I told myself on the way to school the next day.

It was the morning after Jeremy had called me. *Jeremy.* I even liked his name.

I glanced at my watch. It was exactly ten hours and thirty-seven minutes since I had hung up the phone.

What was I going to do? I couldn't stop thinking about him. I felt so . . . well . . . *guilty.*

He was Stacey's boyfriend. I would never try to take him away from her. Would I? What was happening?

I'd have to tell Erica about this.

"Claudia?" Jeremy was standing by the lockers.

"Jeremy," I said. "Hey."

He looked awfully cute.

"Hey."

"So . . ."

"So . . ."

This was the weirdest ten seconds of my entire life. Here I was, standing next to this person I had gabbed on the phone with for almost a whole hour, and we had *nothing* to say?

"Uh, cool outfit." Jeremy pointed to my plaid shirt. I was wearing it with brown bell-bottom pants and maroon sneakers.

"Yours too." He had on a black denim jacket, painter's pants, and Doc Martens.

We stood there for another few seconds, wobbling.

I couldn't look him directly in the eye. He avoided my glances too.

Suddenly, we both said, "Last night — "

We smiled.

"Was fun, really fun," I finished with a sigh.

"I'm glad we can still be friends, Claudia."

"Me too."

Suddenly, I saw Stacey in the distance.

I hope we can still be friends.

Jeremy kept talking to me. He hadn't seen Stacey

yet. But I didn't really hear what he was saying. I was much more focused on Stacey and what *she* was going to do next. Grab Jeremy and run down the hall was my guess.

But she kept her distance. She didn't mow me over to whisk Jeremy away. She didn't interrupt us like she had last week. She waited. She leaned on the lockers and waited until Jeremy walked away. And then she walked up to me.

"I need to talk to you right now," Stacey whispered, grabbing *my* arm this time.

"It's time for class," I said, pulling away.

"This won't take very long."

Exasperated, she led me into the girls' room and checked under each stall to make sure no one else was there.

For a moment, I actually thought she was ready to make up with me. Maybe she was going to call an end to our feud. I felt clammy, tense.

Stacey stood there like a totem pole, but she was staring at the floor and tapping her foot.

Part of me wanted things to be the way they used to be. Another part of me felt a little queasy. And angry. And depressed. And anxious.

Stacey pointed her finger at me. "I know what you're doing, Claudia."

"Huh?"

She was like a boxer ready to pounce on me.

"I know what you're doing! This thing you have going on with Jeremy. I've seen the way you two act together. Look, I told you before that I don't care if you're friends with him. That's fine. But remember that he's *my* boyfriend, okay?"

She'd knocked me out with that one.

"Okay?" she repeated, with her hands on her hips.

I nodded. What could I say?

And then she added, a little bit more softly, "No hard feelings?"

No hard feelings?

With that, she picked up her backpack and walked out of the girls' room.

I grabbed for the edge of the sink so I wouldn't fall over.

My *ex*-best friend had just attacked me at school. She hadn't thrown *real* punches, of course, but her words had hurt just as much.

But remember that he's my *boyfriend, okay?*

I splashed a little cool water on my face.

I couldn't believe the Stacey McGill that I once knew and loved would ever do such a thing. What was going on?

That's when the second bell rang. I took a deep breath. First period would start in less than a minute. I had to hurry. I sped out into the corridor and rushed to English.

Mrs. Hall told us about our new reading assignment: *A Tale of Two Cities* by Charles Dickens. It's a novel about the French Revolution.

Between my English assignment and my confrontation with Stacey, I was facing one battle after another.

I couldn't wait to see Erica to ask her advice on the situation. After school, we headed for a baby-sitting job at the Pikes'.

The Pikes were quiet as mice when we first arrived. I think that because Jordan wanted to impress Erica, he convinced his brothers and sisters to be on their very best behavior. Even though we were sitting for seven kids, it felt like we were watching only one or two.

After awhile, we left all the kids upstairs reading and playing videos, while I spilled my guts out to Erica.

"Stacey said *what*? She did *what*?"

Erica didn't believe me at first. And when I told

her the part about having no hard feelings, Erica just laughed.

"No hard feelings? How about no feelings at all?"

I wanted to cry. After all, Stacey was my best friend. Forever and ever and all that. I couldn't just shut off my feelings for her. And Stacey had feelings too, right? I couldn't believe that she'd suddenly turned into a monster.

"The strange thing is," I said to Erica, "part of me wishes Stacey were here now."

Before I could say anything else, Vanessa appeared.

"Can we have an important meeting, please?"

Vanessa marched into the living room, followed by Nicky and her sisters. They looked serious.

"Ahem. We need to talk to you about . . . well . . ."

"It's just that . . ."

"Claudia, you know we like it when you sit for us, but . . ."

"We like Erica a lot too, but . . ."

Claire spoke up all of a sudden. (She's the youngest Pike.)

"I wanna play with Sta-cey again," she whined, sounding an awful lot like a Rugrat.

It turned out that the kids had heard everything I'd said to Erica. They'd heard what had happened in school between Stacey and me and they didn't like it one bit. Stacey had been their baby-sitter and my friend for a long time. They weren't ready to give up on her.

They were very confused.

"What happened to all the times you guys told us you were friends for life? We believed you," Vanessa said.

Think fast, Claudia. How do you answer that one? Uh, sorry, but Stacey turned into a fink, so . . .

"S-s-s-some best friends have fights," I stammered. "Sometimes friends decide that they want to do different things. They need time apart. What used to be fun isn't fun anymore and . . ."

Was anyone listening? Not really.

That was when Erica stepped in and rescued me.

"You guys! What's the problem? I'm just Erica the baby-sitting *temp*! I'm not here to *replace* anyone."

Claire sniffled. "You're *not*?"

"No. I'm just filling in for a short time while Stacey takes a break. She'll be back. There's absolutely nothing you should worry about."

The Pike kids seemed okay with Erica's answer.

"But when do you think you and Stacey will make up?" Vanessa asked me.

I started to say that I didn't know when.

Then I started to say maybe someday in the near future.

Then . . .

I lost track of what I was saying.

Sorry to break this to you, kids, but I will absolutely, under no circumstances, never, ever, ever be baby-sitting with Stacey McGill again, got it?

They would die if they knew that.

But in the bottom of my soul and in the pit of my stomach, I thought that was true.

Even if I still missed Stacey more than ever before.

✿ Chapter 11

Things I Have to Do Right Now:
1. Finish centerpiece for dinner. (Add feathers to turkey if there's time.)
2. Try again to fix origami turkeys. (They look more like turtles. Should I put them at plates or not? Add them to centerpiece?)
3. Go to cemetery to visit Mimi this week. (Sometimes around the holidays I go visit where she's buried just to say hello and put some evergreen branches by her headstone.)

So now it was Thanksgiving and I hadn't spoken to Stacey (not a surprise) or Jeremy (a little bit of a surprise) in three whole days. After seeing Jeremy in the hall everywhere for an entire week, he seemed to have suddenly disappeared. My theory was that

Stacey was staking out the halls, waiting until I was gone before she let him go to classes.

I missed talking to him, in a friend kind of way.

I had made arrangements to go to Peaches's early to watch the Macy's parade with her, Molly, and Lynn (not that Lynn would actually watch, of course). When I got there, Molly answered the door.

"You must be Claudia," she exclaimed, and threw her arms around me and squeeeeeeezed. Then she called back to Peaches, "She's here! And she's just gorgeous!"

Peaches came into the living room, toting Lynn in one arm and a diaper in her free hand.

"So I see you've met Molly," she said, winking at me.

"Yup, she has! And she is just drop-dead, Miyoshi." (Miyoshi is Peaches' real name.)

I felt my cheeks flush at all this flattery.

"Happy Thanksgiving," I said meekly.

Peaches and Molly looked at each other and laughed. Then we sat on the sofa to watch the parade.

We alternated between watching and talking about Molly's adventures as photographer of the world. She has an *awesome* life. She's seen *everything*. She's done *everything*.

"I was in this little town in Greece a month ago and I had the chance to photograph an exquisite wedding. It was on a cliff near the ocean and it was just breathtaking."

I smiled, but Peaches was frowning. Why?

"That's a far cry from photographing my ordinary Stoneybrook wedding, eh, Molly?" Peaches said.

"What are you talking about, Miyoshi? You and Russ are perfect."

"Photos of our life in Stoneybrook are certainly no match for the ones you've taken in Greece and Sydney and St. Petersburg."

Molly reached for my aunt's hand. "Where is this coming from?"

"Oh, just ignore me. I'm tired, that's all."

I suddenly let out a burst of laughter that cut through the tension.

"Look at Clifford!" I shrieked. On the TV, the Clifford balloon had sprung a leak and its nose was deflating. "The Big Red Dog isn't so big anymore. He's shrinking."

Molly laughed too.

"Hey, Miyoshi, do you remember that time in

college when that professor — oh, what was his name — something like hammer or wrench or — "

"Lugnut?"

"That's it! Lugnut! Remember him? With his big red nose and cheeks? And he was threatening to fail me in chemistry, so you went to his office to complain?"

"You didn't deserve to be failed."

"Yes I did. I stunk in chemistry! Claudia." Molly turned to me. "Your aunt is the truest, bluest friend you would *ever* want to have. You don't find many like her."

Now it was my aunt's turn to blush.

Lynn gurgled.

"See?" Molly continued. "Even Lynn agrees."

I nodded. Of course I agreed too. I thought Peaches was the greatest aunt in the universe.

"Molly, what else did you guys do at school?" I asked.

Molly threw herself back on the couch. "Claudia, I could talk for hours! Don't even get me started."

"She's right," Peaches said. "*Don't* get her started. We'll never get to dinner."

Russ called out from the other room, "Time to hit the road, folks! Time to face the turkey!"

Peaches gathered up Lynn, turned to Molly, and said, "I'm sorry for what I was saying before. It's just that — "

Molly threw her arms around my aunt and said, "Enough. No explanations necessary."

They laughed and hugged, and we left for the Kishi Thanksgiving feast.

On the ride to our house, Molly did most of the talking, reminiscing about old times again with Peaches.

My mind was racing.

I wondered where Stacey was on this day. In New York with her dad? Had she said so at a BSC meeting the week before? I couldn't remember. The events of the last month were a blur to me.

I couldn't help feeling that Stacey and I were a lot like Molly and Peaches. At least we had been before Jeremy. I remembered Peaches' story about Billy Bradford. My aunt and Molly hadn't let a boy come between them. Maybe there was still hope for Stacey and me.

But I doubted it. Stacey wouldn't be coming over after dinner this year. We wouldn't be swapping Thanksgiving stories. We wouldn't be scoping out the post-Thanksgiving sales at Washington Mall.

Not this year. And maybe not ever.

❋ Chapter 12

"We're heeeeeeeere!" Molly sang out as we walked into my house.

My mom had met Molly a few times before. "Molly Bishop, you look great!"

Everyone said their hellos and then we crashed in the living room in front of the television again. It was funny, because I hardly ever watch TV, but on Thanksgiving, between the parade and football, the TV is on all day long. Russ and Dad were placing bets (just for fun, not for money) on which team would win the afternoon game. Meanwhile, I was holding Lynn tightly in my arms. She had almost fallen asleep. I have that effect on babies, I guess.

The dinner hour approached. When it came time to eat, we couldn't sit down fast enough.

"What a beautiful centerpiece!" Molly and Peaches declared.

"And these place cards too. Claudia, these are wonderful," Russ added.

I was proud.

Molly pulled out her camera with its different lenses and flashes. "Photo op!" She took a shot of the table and then turned her camera on me. "Smile, beautiful!"

There were dishes crammed together on a small table at one side of the dining room. I drooled looking at them. There was hot squash, sage stuffing, whipped potatoes, whole-berry cranberry sauce, steaming green beans, and more. Peaches had even baked pumpkin muffins.

"I think now would be a good time to say grace," Dad said. "How about each of us saying something we're grateful for."

Everyone agreed. Dad began.

"On this Thanksgiving, I am thankful for my wonderful wife, my two daughters, and good friends and family."

Janine was next. "I'm grateful for everyone, of course . . . and for life in general."

Mom continued. "I am also thankful for family. I

am truly blessed. And I must admit that I am also thankful that the turkey isn't dry."

Everyone chuckled. Mom turned to Russ.

"Thankful is all I am. Especially today. For my big Peach and my littlest peach, Lynn. And my nieces."

I was starting to feel all warm and fuzzy inside.

Molly spoke up next. "Well, I'm just plain lucky to be here, since my family is overseas and . . . well, being in Stoneybrook is just about the greatest gift I could hope for. You are all a joy. Thanks to all of you for reminding me about the importance of home."

Lynn, in her high chair, gurgled. I think even she was thankful.

Peaches spoke next and got all choked up. She talked about how lucky she was — that lately she had been feeling kind of sad but that those closest to her reminded her she was actually very fortunate.

She winked at me when she said that. Then she blew a kiss to Molly, who smiled.

They looked so happy to be with each other. Even after my aunt's nervousness these two pals really did seem to be there for each other no matter what.

Russ grabbed Peaches and squeezed.

And then it was my turn. "Thank you for this food," I began, sounding as if I were praying. "Thank you for a niece like Lynn. Thanks for a sister like Janine — even when we fight."

I included everyone in the room. And in my mind, I was silently giving thanks for each of my friends. For my newest friend, Erica.

And for my old friend, Stacey, traitor or not.

❋ Chapter 13

"You never go shopping just for fun?" I asked. I couldn't believe it.

Erica and I were taking a walk through downtown Stoneybrook. She and I had talked for a few minutes after the guests had left on Thanksgiving. She wanted to hang out on Friday, but I could tell by the sound of her voice that she wasn't eager to go shopping again.

But we had to go shopping! Everybody goes shopping the day after Thanksgiving.

"Well, we could meet downtown instead of at the mall. It'll be less crowded. Please?" I had said.

After eleven "pleases," Erica finally agreed. We'd meet at eleven o'clock the next day. I was determined to make a post-Thanksgiving shopping spree happen with or without Stacey.

I'd even made a list:

Shopping with Erica

- shoe sale at Bellair's
- pierced ears for Erica?
- pet store
- lunch at Rosebud Cafe

I had closed my eyes, dreaming of sidewalk sales and bargain racks. More than anything else, I wanted Erica to like the same things I liked.

Just like Stacey did.

It wasn't going to be easy, though.

"Well," Erica said, "*some*times I browse in the art store, but no, I have never devoted an entire day to walking around buying things. Not like you."

"Erica," I exclaimed, "you don't always have to *buy*. Window-shop! It's like an art, you know."

"Really? An art?"

I stopped in front of a store window. It was the Connecticut Yankee Shop. Perfect.

"Like here. Check out all these candles."

"Yeah, so?"

"So many colors. So many scents. So many sizes.

I can just imagine all the places I could put them or all the people I could give them to as gifts."

Erica started to wander away while I was talking. I shouted after her. "Hey! Wait up! I was telling you something."

"Oh. I thought you were finished. Can we go somewhere else?"

I frowned. "Okay, you don't like candles. Then how about Bellair's? It's a department store, so you can look at a whole bunch of stuff at once. Plus, they're having this awesome shoe sale."

"Okay. I'll cruise the shoes." Erica laughed at her rhyme.

We headed for the shoe department in Bellair's, gabbing a mile a minute. I mentioned that I hadn't seen Jeremy in a couple of days.

Erica hinted that maybe (just maybe) I liked Jeremy a little more than I wanted to admit.

"No way," I told her. Jeremy Rudolph was strictly off-limits. Stacey had made that perfectly clear.

As we switched escalators to go to a higher floor, Erica told me that she couldn't baby-sit on Sunday for the Pikes. She had a family commitment that she couldn't cancel. Fortunately, she had let Kristy know on Wednesday night. "Kristy said not to worry."

I was bummed out. Kristy would probably take the job herself, which would be fine, but I'd been looking forward to sitting with my new friend again.

"It sure is crowded in here," Erica noticed, glancing at the row of shoppers lined up behind us on the escalator.

"You know," I said, "when Stacey and I used to come to Bellair's after Thanksgiving, we would actually get up early in the morning to try to be first in line. Can you believe that?"

Erica just looked at me. "Yeah?"

"And there was one Thanksgiving when Stacey got into an argument with this other girl we know. They both saw a pair of bargain shoes at the same time. It was funny because the two of them each had one shoe in her hand and — "

"You know, Claudia," Erica interrupted, "maybe shopping wasn't such a good idea. And I don't really *need* any shoes."

"But you just said a minute ago that — "

"I know you want to go shoe shopping. That's cool. But maybe I'll go to the music section or the book section, okay? I'm sorry. I know you and Stacey used to have fun doing this together but . . ."

I told her we could skip the shoes. The whole

idea of the day was to spend time together, not to buy shoes.

"How about the jewelry department downstairs?" I asked.

"I told you at the mall that I'm not really into jewelry."

"*Please*? Just for two seconds." I nudged her on the shoulder and whined, "Pleeeeeeeeeease?"

She laughed and agreed to go.

Once we were there, I think Erica was surprised by how much fun we had at the earring counter. I worked my shopping charms and convinced her to try on a few pairs. The woman behind the register helped us pick out different styles and colors — all clip-on earrings, since Erica refused to get her ears pierced. They were having a sale — buy two pairs and get one free.

"I have to admit that these would look nice on me," Erica said, admiring a pair of dainty fake-diamond earrings in the mirror. "I never would have guessed it."

"You absolutely sparkle, dah-ling," I purred. A saleswoman with bright red lipstick was pulling other earrings off the rack for Erica to look at.

"Buy two pairs, get one free," I reminded her.

Erica was actually having a good time shopping, and it was all thanks to me! Inside Erica's cynical shell was a shopper just waiting to come out.

The saleswoman handed Erica a pair of garnet drop earrings. "Now, these would look lovely with your hair. They would pick up the red highlights."

Erica's hair looked brown to me, but she bought the saleslady's line anyway. After a few minutes, to my great surprise, Erica was ready to buy *both* pairs.

"I love garnets," she declared. "I love the color. These really do match my hair."

The saleswoman beamed.

"You know something funny?" I said to Erica. "Stacey loves that stone too. She has a garnet ring that her dad got for her in New York, and when we were shopping there once we actually — "

Erica cut me off. "Hey! You know what? Why don't *you* get the free pair?"

"Me?"

"I absolutely never would have tried on earrings if it hadn't been for you. And I love these. So you take the free pair, okay?"

I nodded and picked out a pair of silver hoops with little green beads on them. They would go perfectly with my green turtleneck sweater. I'd wear them to school on Monday.

"Thanks so much, Erica. These are awesome."

Erica decided to wear the garnet earrings out of the store. Slowly, before my very eyes, she was becoming (dare I say it?) *fashionable*.

After that, we shopped everywhere. Erica changed her mind and agreed to go back to the shoe sale. We even tried on some hats in one of Bellair's new basement boutiques.

"Where to now?" Erica asked as we left Bellair's.

"I don't know, Stace."

Erica stopped short. "What did you say?"

I realized that I had just called Erica "Stace."

"Did you just call me *Stace*?" Erica asked.

"No, I — " I tried hard to change the subject.

"Let's just eat," said Erica.

Why had I called her Stace?

A moment later, we were entering the Rosebud Cafe. After an awkward silence, Erica had perked up.

"I know it's cold outside," she said as we entered the restaurant, "but I am going to have a strawberry milk shake anyway."

The place was packed, but a waitress led us to a table after about five minutes. She motioned to the back room for a busboy to clear up the plates left by the last customers.

I looked up and saw a familiar face.

"Logan?"

The busboy for our table was Logan Bruno. As he collected cups and saucers he explained that the "Road Spud" (that's what he calls the restaurant sometimes) was always busiest around the holidays.

"So what's up?" I asked him. I hadn't seen much of him lately.

"Well, Mary Anne and I broke up, remember?" He grabbed the bus tray and backed away. "Happy Thanksgiving — a day late. See you around."

Uh-oh. Logan looked unhappy and he sounded miserable.

I told Erica about the Logan and Mary Anne situation. She was very sympathetic and reminded me of Peaches, since she knew how to say the right thing at the right time.

We ordered the milk shakes, fries, and burgers. Everything was yummy. I had eaten so much food in the last two days.

"I am STUFFED," Erica pronounced, patting her belly, as the waiter took our dishes away.

I grinned. "Stacey used to make this joke all the time about having a big belly like Santa at the holidays. She said — "

I looked up and saw Erica's face cloud over.

"What?" I said. "What is it?"

"I just can't compete, Claudia."

"What do you mean?"

"I can't compete with Stacey. I'm not her, Claudia. If you want to be with Stacey, then you should call her up. Not me. I want to be myself. I don't want to be the friend you take shopping on the rebound."

"It's not like that!" I protested. "What are you talking about? I don't want to be with Stacey. I want to be with *you*."

"Yeah, sure. That's why you keep telling me Stacey stories and wondering where Stacey is. You even called me Stace by mistake. I'm tired of this. I was just starting to like shopping, even though I never thought I would. But you're not here with *me*. You're thinking about Stacey."

"No I'm not — "

Erica stood up in a huff. Then she carefully took off the garnet earrings and placed them on the table in front of me.

"Claudia, take these back. I don't want them."

"I can't take them *back*. . . ."

"Then give them to Stacey. They'll go with her ring. I don't wear earrings, remember?"

Erica dug out a wrinkled ten-dollar bill from her

wallet and left without even saying good-bye. She just dropped the earrings, paid her part of the check, and walked away.

And I didn't run after her.

Maybe she wasn't such a great friend after all. Or maybe I wasn't.

❋ Chapter 14

I realized something interesting yesterday.

Friends are not necessarily forever.

Yesterday I did the following things in this order:

1. slept
2. ate a turkey sandwich
3. did a little math homework
4. slept some more
5. drew a picture of Lynn from a photo on my desk

I felt like a robot going through the motions, not like Claudia Kishi the artist. I was so tired of being upset. I wanted my average life back.

I wanted to call Erica but I couldn't. What could I possibly say to make up for what had happened? How could I explain calling her by the wrong name?

Everything was a mess.

The members of the BSC got together last night. Actually, they got together on Friday night, with Stacey, but I couldn't go because I was with Erica. So they got together *again* (minus Stacey) to see me on Saturday. Everywhere I turned, there was another reminder of the fact that I was in the middle of a Friendship Feud . . . or two. I felt ninety-nine percent guilty and depressed, one percent good.

Well, maybe better than that. I admit that Saturday evening was fun. Mal, Jessi, Kristy, Abby, and Mary Anne hung out at my house. It seemed like old times, as if we were having a BSC meeting in my bedroom. We even flipped through an old appointment book and started to remember funny sitting jobs. Jessi and Mallory hadn't seen each other much in the past few months, so they were particularly thrilled to be there, chatting in the corner of the room about writing and dance.

I told Mallory about Jordan and Erica — how Erica had gotten him to chill out and do his homework. We laughed about boyfriends, avoiding the subjects of Logan and Jeremy. I decided my friends had probably had an earful about the big J the night before with Stacey. I was not prepared to admit anything about my feelings concerning Jeremy or Stacey.

Every time I mentioned either of them, it got me into trouble.

And here I was, on Sunday, still feeling like a heel.

Today Mal was heading back to Riverbend with her family, and I was going to baby-sit for the Pike kids while they drove her there. Now I was glad I wouldn't be sitting with Erica. How embarrassing that would have been.

When I knocked on the Pikes' door, Claire pulled it open, wearing a semitoothless grin (she'd lost a front tooth on Thanksgiving).

"Claudia!" she said, smiling from ear to ear and reaching out for a hug.

I stepped inside the house and saw the other kids behind Claire. Poised in a neat row on the sofa, the Pikes were sitting up straight like birds on a wire.

Sitting in a chair, not too far away, was Stacey.

"Hi, Stacey." I spoke up first. "I can't believe Kristy called *you* to baby-sit."

"Kristy?" Stacey repeated. "Kristy didn't call me."

Vanessa blushed and started to walk out of the room.

"Vanessaaaaaaaaah?" I called after her. "Vanessa

Pike, you wouldn't have anything to do with this, would you?"

She slouched back into the living room, then stood, rocking back and forth on her heels.

"Vanessa?" I said again.

Vanessa squirmed. "Kristy told Mom she was going to sit, but we said we wanted Stacey, and Kristy said it was okay to call her, so Mom did."

I rolled my eyes.

"Claudia, does it really matter why I'm here?" Stacey said with an impatient sigh. "Let's just do this, okay?"

Last week in school she had told me off and now she was pretending it was okay. She was telling me what to do, just like she had done in the girls' room.

"All right. I'll go see what the triplets are doing."

But the Pike girls pulled me back into the living room. They wouldn't let me get away from Stacey.

The next hour was the longest (and quietest) I've ever spent in the Pike household. The only thing that the youngest Pikes wanted to do was sit on the edge of the sofa and watch Stacey and me.

What was going on?

Stacey glanced at me. No matter how hard either of us tried, the Pikes seemed determined to keep us . . .

Together.

How could I have missed something so obvious?

Suddenly the pieces of the puzzle snapped into place.

"Okay, kids," I said. "Go read. Go do homework. Go do something. Time to leave Stacey and me alone."

On their way out of the room, I could detect sneaky smiles on their faces.

Stacey flopped onto the couch. "Claudia, why are we doing this?"

"Why are we doing what?"

"Why are we fighting like this?"

"I don't know. You tell me."

"Claudia, we've been friends forever."

All of the butterflies that had been whirring around inside my stomach suddenly stopped. "I know we have," I said.

"So why are we still fighting? It just seems so . . . so . . ."

"Dumb?" I asked.

"Yeah. I mean, I forgive you for telling Jeremy about Ethan . . ."

Wait a minute. What did she say? She forgives *me*?

"I know you didn't mean to tattle on me," she

went on. "Plus, I really think that since our talk on Monday you've been great about staying away from Jeremy."

"Gee, Stacey, I don't know if — "

"You know, Claud, I don't think I've seen you and Jeremy together all week. That really takes a load off my mind."

I was speechless.

"Isn't it funny, Claud, that we could have had this kind of misunderstanding? And over a boy too. We said we'd never, ever do that, remember? You know, I really miss you."

I wanted to tell her that I missed her too. That I went shopping and found the garnet earrings, and that I never, ever wanted to fight over a boy.

"Stacey, I missed you too," I confessed. I couldn't help myself.

She smiled and reached out to give me a hug.

I was relieved. Was Stacey back? I wanted my best friend back.

"I'm so glad you said something, Stace, because I have been thinking about our friendship all week. All month!"

"Me too."

"I didn't have the courage to tell you this before — "

"We have the Jeremy thing behind us, right?" Stacey looked into my eyes. "You're going to avoid him in school like I said, right? I mean, maybe we can hang out together as friends, but I don't know about that just yet. In a little while . . ."

"What are you talking about?"

"Jeremy. Remember?"

"Wait just a minute. This is about you and Jeremy? What about you and *me*?"

"What about us? We just made up."

I shook my head. I was *not* going to let her get away with this. "*You* just made up, Stacey. I barely got to say anything."

"You said you missed me."

"I *do* miss you. But you said some really mean things to me."

"I was feeling protective, that's all."

"About what? About who? Don't you trust me?"

Stacey paused. "Yeah, I guess so. Most of the time."

I couldn't believe we were having this conversation. "Stacey, don't you get it?"

"I guess not."

"When I say I missed you — I *really* missed you. And I wouldn't *steal* your boyfriend. Friends don't do that to each other. No matter what they feel."

"And what do you feel, Claudia?"

"Hurt."

"I said I was sorry. Can't we just forget it and go back?"

"Go back?"

"To the way it was. To the mall. Hanging out in your room. You know, I thought of you all during Thanksgiving dinner. I was going to even call you, but — "

"But you didn't."

"No . . ."

"I'll bet you called Jeremy, though."

Stacey didn't answer that. Obviously, she was feeling guilty — and I wanted her to feel guilty. I wanted her to feel lonely and sad, like I'd been feeling all weekend.

"Claudia, I just want to be your best friend." She was starting to cry.

"You should have thought of that before, Stacey."

"But I thought you said you missed me — "

I had to hold my breath to keep from crying too.

That's when Vanessa rushed into the living room, screaming.

Frodo was loose again, but I had a sneaking suspicion someone had helped him to get loose. The Pike kids knew we were fighting. Their plan A had backfired. Time for plan B.

I guessed that Vanessa had heard everything. Stacey starting to cry, me starting to yell . . . and had rushed in to interrupt us.

Out of the corner of my eye, I saw Frodo dash under the sofa.

"Come here, you little rodent!" I said, and hit the floor, hands poking around for the energetic ball of fluff.

After all the commotion had passed, I returned him safely to his cage. By this time, Stacey had wiped away her tears so the kids wouldn't see that she'd been crying. She was talking to Vanessa about school and TV while they straightened up the living room.

What had just happened?

Stacey had tried to apologize. But that was no apology. In any case, do real friends forbid you to talk to their boyfriends? I hadn't realized Stacey was so insecure. But she was.

If only she had trusted me.

If only she were more like Erica.

Erica?

I suddenly realized that I had made a big mistake.

Everything made sense now. I had thought I wanted to be best friends with Stacey again, but what I really wanted was for Stacey and me to be the way we used to be together.

I took another deep breath because now it was impossible to hold back the tears.

I had spent so much time obsessing about Stacey that I had overlooked someone else who was a much better friend to me. Someone who listened, who cared, and who even *shopped* — just for me. I had been wrong. I didn't want Erica to be more like Stacey.

I wanted Stacey to be more like Erica.

I owed Erica the biggest apology.

I would NOT lose two friends in one week.

❀ Chapter 15

After leaving the Pikes', I dashed over to Peaches's house to say good-bye to Molly, who was taking off on a business trip to Japan. Her Thanksgiving visit was almost over.

"I wish I could go to Japan with you," I said wistfully. "I could meet some of the other people in our family."

Molly smiled. "I'm afraid my suitcase is already stuffed to the gills. I'd never be able to squeeze you in." She turned to Lynn, who was wriggling around in Peaches' arms. "But you, little peach, would fit *perfectly*. Hey, Miyoshi, are you sure I can't borrow the baby . . . just for awhile?"

Peaches handed Lynn to me and wrapped her arms tightly around Molly's shoulders as they said good-bye.

"You've already had my entire family on loan for a week — what more do you want?" Peaches asked.

"I wouldn't mind having your life, I'll tell you that."

Molly promised that she would try harder to write and that she'd send along all of her Thanksgiving photos as soon as they were developed.

On her way to the airport, Peaches dropped me off at Erica's house. I was ready to apologize. I had called ahead so Erica was prepared. I was coming with a peace offering.

The minute Erica opened the door, I started my apology. "I am sorry for everything that happened on Friday. Really sorry."

"Claudia, look — "

"No, no. Let me finish. Stacey is the only best friend I've ever had. When I think about things to do with a best friend, I think of stuff I did with *her*. I don't want you to be like Stacey. I just want you to be you. In fact, I wish Stacey were more like you."

"Oh, Claudia," said Erica. "I forgave you on Friday night."

"You did? On *Friday*?"

"Yeah. I just lost my temper. I'm sorry too. I'm sorry about you and Stacey. I guess I got a little jealous, though."

"Jealous?"

"I felt like I couldn't compete with someone you've known for so long. I've only been your friend for a week."

"So you're not mad at me?"

Erica laughed. "Of course not. How about coming in out of the cold?" Erica held the door open for me. "Let's just keep the shopping trips to a minimum, okay? Come on in and I'll make some hot chocolate."

I perked up. "Hot chocolate? Ooooh, I hope it's the kind with the teeny marshmallows in it."

It was. We hung out for an hour or two in her basement. Her parents had put a couple of old chairs and a sofa there and turned it into a recreation room. *It would be fun to hang out here more often*, I thought.

I was definitely planning to do that.

The next morning, I was dreading school more than usual. I didn't want to run into Stacey just yet. (I hadn't even thought about what I would do at the BSC meeting later that afternoon.)

But Erica calmed me down.

I had to walk three blocks out of my way to go to SMS via Erica's house, but I did it anyway. I returned the garnet earrings to her and put on the silver hoops I had gotten for free. We both looked mah-vel-ous! Then Erica even let me help fix her hair.

When we got to school, we said good-bye at the lockers and made plans to meet at lunchtime.

"Save me a seat!" I called after her.

"That's what friends are for," she sang back to me.

I laughed.

As I headed to class, I realized that I had forgotten about the reading assignment in *A Tale of Two Cities*. But before I could get too upset, I saw Jeremy standing outside the classroom.

"Hey, Claudia."

"Hey, Jeremy."

"Is this your English class?" he asked me, pointing to Mrs. Hall's door.

I nodded.

"Mine too," he said. "I just got switched into it."

He smiled.

I smiled.

Coincidence?

Maybe.

Monday morning was turning out to be very interesting.

Ann M. Martin

About the Author

ANN MATTHEWS MARTIN was born on August 12, 1955. She grew up in Princeton, NJ, with her parents and her younger sister, Jane.

Although Ann used to be a teacher and then an editor of children's books, she's now a full-time writer. She gets ideas for her books from many different places. Some are based on personal experiences. Others are based on childhood memories and feelings. Many are written about contemporary problems or events.

All of Ann's characters, even the members of the Baby-sitters Club, are made up. (So is Stoneybrook.) But many of her characters are based on real people. Sometimes Ann names her characters after people she knows; other times she chooses names she likes.

In addition to the Baby-sitters Club books, Ann Martin has written many other books for children. Her favorite is *Ten Kids, No Pets* because she loves big families and she loves animals. Her favorite BSC book is *Kristy's Big Day*. (Kristy is her favorite baby-sitter.)

Ann M. Martin now lives in New York with her cats, Gussie, Woody, and Willy, and her dog, Sadie. Her hobbies are reading, sewing, and needlework — especially making clothes for children.

Look for #5

KRISTY POWER!

Oh, yeah. This was Cary's room all right. There was no mistaking it. Who else would have a poster of the universe with a little YOU ARE HERE arrow pointing to Earth? Who else would have a weird painting of clocks melting all over the place? (Claudia told me later that it was probably by a guy named Salvador Dalí, who was famous for "surreal" paintings.) Or one of a man with a big green apple for a head? (That was by Magritte, according to Claudia. Also a surrealist.)

A bulletin board over his desk was covered with funny postcards, bizarre newspaper headlines ("Goat Responsible for Power Outage," said one), and cut-out pictures of movie monsters. It was quite a display.

I turned around slowly, taking in the room. His green plaid bedspread and curtains looked relatively normal, but the lamp on his bedside table was pure Cary. It was a miniature skeleton with a lightbulb held high in one hand.

I looked back at the bulletin board. I had to admit that it was pretty cool. Then my glance dropped to his desk. On top was an open notebook. I figured Cary must have started his homework while I interviewed his brothers. I bent over to look at it, wondering if he'd figured out how to do the math problems we'd been assigned that day.

It wasn't his homework.

It was more like a journal.

And once I started reading, I couldn't stop.

Check out what's new with your old friends.